Cathy Cassidy

the
chocolate
box
Secrets

Perfect presents and
cool fashion makes
for all year round...

PUFFIN BOOKS

UK | USA | Canada | Ireland | Australia
India | New Zealand | South Africa

Puffin Books is part of the Penguin Random House group of companies
whose addresses can be found at global.penguinrandomhouse.com.

puffinbooks.com

Penguin
Random House
UK

First published 2015
001

Text copyright © Cathy Cassidy, 2015
Illustrations copyright © Erin Keen, 2015
Text design and layout by nicandlou

The moral right of the author and illustrator has been asserted

Printed in Great Britain by Clays Ltd, St Ives plc

A CIP catalogue record for this book is available from the British Library

ISBN: 978–0–141–36258–8
www.greenpenguin.co.uk

Thank You . . .

Special thanks to my fab editor, Amanda, and all at Puffin Towers who have made this book possible . . . It's a bit of a labour of love for me, and it means a lot to see the book taking shape! Thanks to Carmen, Nikki, Carolyn, Julia, Sam and the always-fabulous Puffin team. Thanks also to Mary-Jane for her eagle-eyed editing, reader Hannah O for the inspiration behind the awesome Skye's the Limit Birthday Cake and the amazing Erin for her beautiful, beautiful artwork. As always, I'm grateful to my fab family for putting up with me during the writing and editing process, especially my daughter Cait who helped me trial some of the projects. I guess the final thank-you goes to you, my readers . . . for believing in Tanglewood and the world of the Chocolate Box Girls and wanting it to be a little more real. I hope this book will bring the magic closer still . . .

Cathy Cassidy
x
x
♡

Contents

Autumn

Coco says... 68

Winter 114

Meet the Sisters ...

COCO TANBERRY

I'm the youngest of the sisters, although sometimes I think I am way more sensible than the others. They'd disagree — they think I am eccentric and animal crazy, but so what? I can't help it if the world is a mess — but I am determined to save it, preferably with the help of panda cupcakes. I play violin (nobody appreciates my talent, alas) and I have a pony called Caramel, a sheep called Humbug, a dog called Fred and a whole bunch of runner ducks. My best friend is Lawrie Marshall. He's cute — but don't tell him I said so!

Skye Tanberry

Summer and I are identical twins - we come right in the middle of the family, between Honey and Coco. As twins go, we're very close but also quite different. I am kind of obsessed with history and vintage stuff; the past seems like a very cool and magical place, and vintage clothes carry a bit of that magic with them. When I'm older, I'd like to work in costume design - that's my dream. I don't have a boyfriend, though I used to have a long-distance romance with a boy called Jamie Finch.

Summer Tanberry

I'm Skye's twin, but I agree — we're different! My biggest passion is dance, but a couple of years ago I messed up big time when I had the chance to audition for a boarding ballet school. I put myself under way too much pressure and lost the plot for a while. Let's just say I had some eating issues. These days I'm loads better and I try to eat healthily — who doesn't — but I also have a passion for baking! I have a boyfriend, Alfie Anderson. He has stuck by me through the tough times and I love him to bits!

Honey Tanberry

OK, so I have a reputation; people say I am a drama queen, a troublemaker. Really? Me? Nah, I'm just a bit impulsive and I don't like rules much, but trouble? I have had enough of that to last me a lifetime. It sounds cheesy, but you learn from your mistakes and I am trying hard to get my life on track again. I love art, crafts and fashion and I plan to go to art college one day - possibly in Australia, because my boyfriend, Ash, lives there.

Cherry says...

When I first came to Tanglewood I felt like the odd one out; I was used to our family being just Dad and me. Now, though, I can't imagine being anywhere else, and I think the world of my stepsisters. I am even getting used to Honey! We didn't get off to the best of starts because I fell in love with her boyfriend, Shay Fletcher. Shay and I are still together, and Honey and I are finally learning to get along. I may not be great at baking or crafts like the others, but I love to write and my ambition is to be a novelist one day. Stories are everywhere; capturing them and pinning them down on paper is my favourite thing in the world.

Before you start...

A few words of advice

* If you are going to try some of the crafts, recipes and fashion-makes in this book, check before you start that you have everything you need for the project.
* If you're baking or cooking, assemble all the ingredients and cooking utensils you need before you start and make sure you stay in the kitchen to keep an eye on what you're making. Kitchen disasters will not make you popular!
* Always have an adult around to supervise any kitchen activities that involve boiling or simmering liquids, e.g. melting chocolate over a pan of simmering water, making toffee, etc. Better safe than sorry!
* Lots of the craft projects involve a bit of recycling, which is very cool, but don't get too keen and try to recycle something your family still want or need! If in doubt, always ask first.
* Use an apron or an old shirt to cover your clothes when you are doing anything messy, whether it's craft or kitchen-based.

A few crafty staples to keep in stock

* A SMALL HOT-MELT GLUE GUN (sounds scary but really isn't and can be bought cheaply from a craft shop or online). Until you are used to it, ask an adult to supervise when you are using it. The glue is very hot initially and you need to get into the habit of making sure you don't let it touch your skin. Alternatively, you can use superglue or any other strong glue when a hot glue gun is required, but again, get parental supervision and be careful!
* A BOTTLE OF WHITE PVA GLUE AND A GLUE STICK (both will be very useful!)
* SCISSORS have at least two pairs of biggish scissors: one to use solely for fabric, another pair just for paper (these will get blunt more quickly, and you need sharp scissors for fabric).
* NEEDLES, THREAD, EMBROIDERY THREAD, YARN OFFCUTS, GOLD/ SILVER CORD OR THREAD.
* A RAG-BAG where you keep felt and fabric offcuts, lace trim, ribbon, raffia, buttons.

GLOSSARY: SOME ITEMS YOU MAY NOT HAVE COME ACROSS YET!

- **ACETATE** – a type of strong plastic sheeting, available in various sizes from any art or craft shop

- **ACRYLIC PAINT** – available from all good art shops

- **CROCHET HOOK** – like a knitting needle but smaller and with a hooked end, used to crochet; available from wool shops or haberdashery departments

- **EMBROIDERY HOOP** – a small wooden or plastic double-hoop, which stretches fabric to allow you to make fancy embroidery stitches; available from wool shops, haberdashery departments or craft suppliers

- **IRIDESCENT CELLOPHANE** – a gorgeous shimmery kind of cellophane available from art shops and craft suppliers

- **KAPOK** – a type of stuffing used in craft projects; available from craft suppliers

- **PINKING SHEARS** – special scissors that make a serrated cut, either for decoration or to stop fabric from fraying; available from craft suppliers or haberdashery departments

- **RAFFIA** – natural-fibre ribbon-like material, great for craft projects and available in bundles from craft suppliers; comes in natural beige shade or bright/metallic colours

- **RICRAC** – a wiggly braid trim, available by the metre from haberdashery departments

- **WADDING** – a sort of padding material useful in some craft projects, or for stuffing; available by the metre from haberdashery departments or craft suppliers

SUM

MER

Summer is the best time ever at Tanglewood. We have a beach right on our doorstep and that makes us party central all the way through the holidays! I am a bit of a sun-worshipper, and I loved the heat and that whole outdoor living thing when I stayed with Dad in Sydney, but stay-at-home summers can be just as awesome. Everyone seems happier in the sun — and of course, for six whole weeks, there's no school! The days seem to stretch out forever, filled with endless possibilities, and I for one plan to make the most of every minute!

Here are just a few of the things we get up to . . .

Honey
xx

A Sweet Summer Sleepover

Cherry says...

The first summer I came to Tanglewood, we had a Chocolate Festival, and it was just the coolest thing ever.

OK, so not every village has a food festival for you to join in with, and not everyone's dad and stepmum run a chocolate business, but you could use these ideas to throw a very cool chocolate-themed sleepover to celebrate the arrival of summertime!

Get organized. How many people will you invite? Will your sleepover be indoors? Outdoors? What if it rains? Plan your decorations and get them made well in advance - they're half the fun!

Try these ideas

1 Decorate your own chocolate cupcakes

Buy ready-made cupcakes and buttercream icing, icing pens and all kinds of sprinkles.

5 Chocolate theme the food

Cake, traybakes (see my recipe, page 206), choc milkshakes, hot chocolates (see Honey's recipe, page 160).

6 Curl up with a film

Chocolat; Charlie and the Chocolate Factory; Forrest Gump ('Life is like a box of chocolates').

2 Chocolate dares

Lucky dip! Pick a wrapped truffle from a hat – each truffle has a dare attached, and you have to do the dare to get the chocolate. Wrap and write the dares beforehand – make sure they're fun or silly.

7 Take over the kitchen and make your own chocolate truffles

(See Paddy's recipe, page 140). You might be too chocolated-out by then to eat them, so pop the truffles in party bags for your guests to take home.

3

Get a drama-mad friend to dress up as a fortune teller and guess your chocolate fortunes. (See next page.)

4 Taste test

Supply lots of different kinds of choc bar, line them up and label them A, B, C, etc., and hide the wrappers. (Don't forget to make a note of which is which first!) Ask your testers to identify the bars and choose their faves.

Chocolate Fortunes

PALM READING WITH A CHOCOLATE TWIST

It is traditional to read the left hand. First, familiarize yourself with the lines, and study each one at a time to give your reading.

The Life Line

- **Long and deep:** health conscious — chocolate is just an occasional treat for you.
- **Small and close to thumb:** don't rely on chocolate too much for an energy boost!
- **Short and shallow:** you'll try anything once!
- **Straight rather than curved:** you prefer the classics when it comes to chocolate.
- **A break in the line:** one day you may go off chocolate altogether.

The Head Line

- **Deep, long line:** you have a few all-time faves and stay loyal to them!
- **Wavy:** fickle and changeable!
- **Crosses on the line:** big decisions to be made. Strawberry cream or nut cluster?
- **Short:** you live in the moment — eat chocolate now and don't think of the consequences!

The Heart Line

- **Strong line starting from index finger:** you're confident, happy and sweet as chocolate.
- **Starts under middle finger:** you can be selfish with your chocolate.
- **Wavy:** you can never pick a favourite choc and always want what others have!
- **Short and straight:** chocolate? You can take it or leave it.

Hand Shape

- **Broad, square hands and short fingers:** practical and sensible, you go for milk chocolate bars from your fave brands.
- **Long fingers and short, narrow hands:** clever and daring, you'll buy Fairtrade dark chocolate in new and risky flavours!
- **Long palm and fingers:** shy and creative, you like truffles — rich, comforting and lots of choice.
- **Long, boxy palm with shorter fingers:** you're drawn to expensive brands.

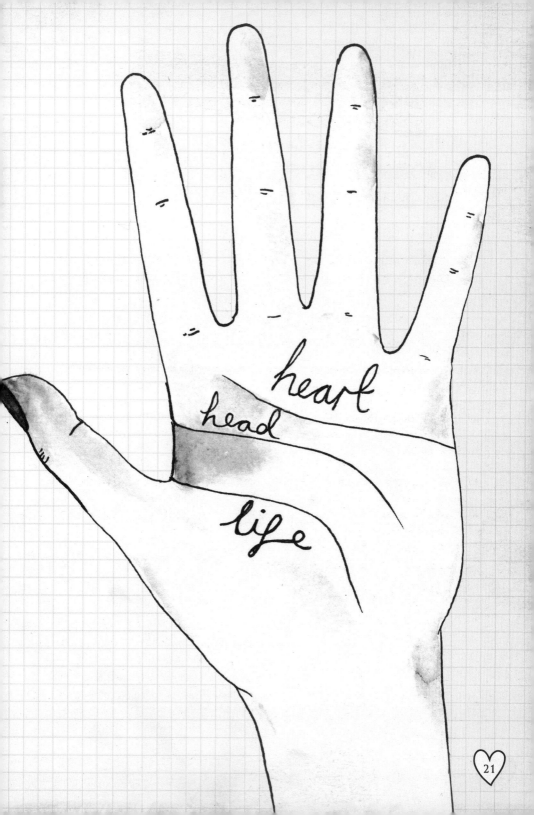

heart

head

life

21

INVENT YOUR OWN
CHOCOLATE TRUFFLES
AND DESIGN THE BOX!

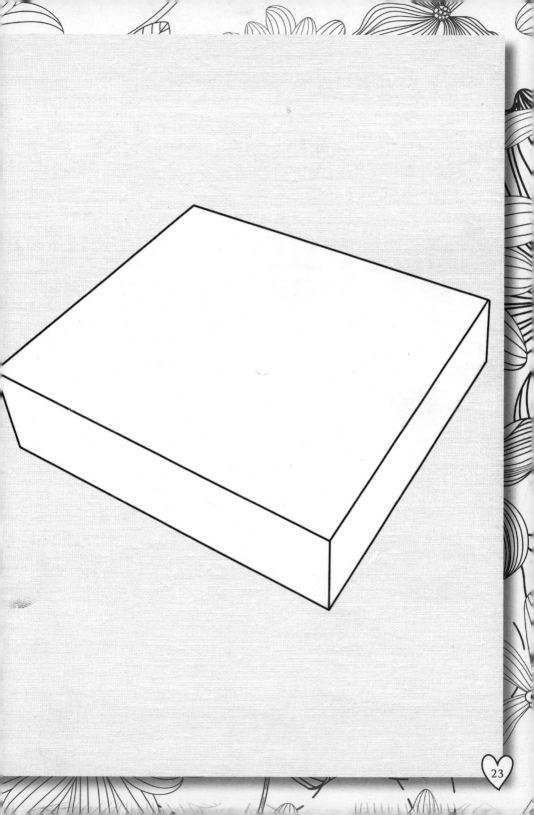

Flower Crown Hairband

Honey says...

Nothing says summertime like a flower crown hairband; I love the look because it has a cool festival vibe and makes loose, unstyled hair look awesome. You don't have to spend a fortune on a flower crown from a fashion store, either - making your own is easy!

YOU WILL NEED:

- an old hairband (plain plastic or fabric covered)
- a hot-melt glue gun or strong glue
- a needle and thread
- fabric scissors
- thin, gauzy or silky fabric in pastel shades
- dark green felt

TO MAKE:

1 Cut petal shapes from the fabric using the template below as a guide.

2 Arrange and twist the petals, layering them to create a flower shape. When you are happy with the shape, make some stitches at the base of the petals to hold them in place.

3 Tweak the flower, folding over some of the petals for a more natural look.

PETAL TEMPLATE

PLEASE PHOTOCOPY ME

FOR A CHEAT'S NO-SEW VERSION, USE
BLOBS OF GLUE TO LAYER THE PETALS AND
GIVE A LITTLE TWIST TO THE FINISHED
FLOWER TO CREATE A RUFFLED EFFECT

VARIATIONS

4 Cut a few leaf shapes and stitch them to some of the flowers.

5 Arrange the flowers in a line until you are happy with the order of shapes and colours.

6 Use a hot-melt glue gun (or strong glue) to attach the flowers to the hairband.

7 If you're using a fabric-covered hairband as a base, you can stitch the flowers on if you prefer.

♥ BRAIDED HIPPIE HEADBAND:

Make a simple plaited headband by braiding together three long strips of fabric or thin ribbon.

Then simply knot the ribbon at the back of your head and allow the ends to trail down your back like streamers.

♥ VINTAGE VIBE:

If you have an offcut of cool embroidered fabric or a piece of vintage lace trim, cut it into a rectangle the size of a broad ribbon and hem neatly if necessary.

Firmly stitch a length of elastic to each end of your vintage fabric to make a circular band which will fit your head.

Smoothie Recipes

Summer says ...

Smoothies are the perfect summer drink. They are so easy to make, and loads of fun! Ideal for an energy-burst breakfast, a quenching cool drink when revising in the garden or even a fun DIY sleepover activity. They don't just taste awesome; they are really good for you too! I've shared some of my best recipes here — they make either one huge drink or two small ones — but the best thing about smoothies is that you don't always need a recipe; you can experiment with whichever fruits you have and add plain yoghurt, milk or coconut milk for an extra rich smoothie.

Cherry Crush

You will need:

- 300g frozen cherries, pitted
- 350ml fat-free plain yoghurt
- 2 tablespoons clear honey

Method:

Place all the ingredients in the blender and scoosh together. If it seems too thick, add a little milk to thin it out and whizz again.

Banana-rama

You will need:
- 2 bananas
- 300ml coconut milk (or cow's milk if you prefer)
- 2 tablespoons peanut butter (optional)

Method:
Chop the bananas, place them in the blender with the coconut milk and whizz until smooth. We all love peanut butter so I've adapted this recipe by adding two tablespoonfuls – it adds protein and tastes great! So add the peanut butter if you like and whizz again. Serve with ice cubes.

Very Berry

You will need:
- 1 small banana
- 150g mixed berries (blackberries, blueberries blackcurrants, raspberries)
- 300ml apple juice
- clear honey

Method:
Slice the banana into the blender, add the berries and a little apple juice, and whizz until smooth, adding more apple juice if needed to make a smooth mixture. Serve with a drizzle of clear honey.

Make a Vintage Top

Skye says...

I love vintage style, but it doesn't have to be all about finding the perfect 1950s sundress or copying the style of a particular decade down to the very last detail. I mean, don't get me wrong, those things can be a lot of fun, but vintage is for everyone and there are lots of easy ways to upcycle and add a little bit of vintage character to your look.

YOU WILL NEED:

- old T-shirts or vest tops, plain (ransack wardrobe or try jumble sales and charity shops)
- fabric scissors, pins, a needle and thread
- old crochet lace doilies, cotton lace fabric or trim (again, try jumble sales or charity shops)
- Plastic beads (optional)

Simple Fringy Top

TO MAKE:

1 This project will show you just how easy upcycling can be! Take a T-shirt or vest top and carefully cut a new neckline — a wide, boat-neck shape. Discard the ribbed neck.

2 Snip a fringe along the hem of the top and wear it with shorts for a cool, casual summer look that will take you anywhere.

3 Thread plastic beads on to the ends of the fringing and knot to secure them if you like; this adds a 70s hippy-chick vibe!

★ Lace-back Top

TO MAKE:

1 A circular lacy doily – the kind used on cake plates or on shelves in days gone by – can add gorgeous detail to a plain white T-shirt. First, cut away the original neck and neaten the new, wider neckline with a lace trim.

2 Cut out a paper pattern using a plate as a guide. The pattern should be a little smaller than the lace circle, allowing a border of 1–2cm all round.

All done! Super pretty!

3 Pin the paper pattern on to the back of the T-shirt and cut out a circle of fabric (being careful not to cut into the front of the T-shirt).

4 Pin the lace doily over the circular hole, arranging it so it looks even all round. Stitch it carefully into place, keeping your stitches very small so they are not too visible.

YOU CAN STITCH RICRAC, BRAID TRIM OR LACE ON TO THE EDGE OF YOUR T-SHIRT

Your space . . .

DESIGN A SUMMER
DRESS MADE FROM
RECYCLED MATERIALS

Chocolate Fondue

Method:

1. Place all the ingredients in a saucepan and heat gently.
2. Stir with a wooden spoon until the chocolate is melted and the mixture is smooth and glossy.
3. Pour the mixture into a fondue pot over a night-light flame or into a warmed dish to serve, and get dipping!

You will need:

- 120ml double cream
- 200g milk chocolate
- 40g butter
- 150ml milk

Get dipping!

To dip:

- strawberries, raspberries, blueberries, chopped banana, apple slices, pineapple chunks

- grapes, melon slices, kiwi fruit chunks

- marshmallows (veggie if you can get them); toast them first for a messy but awesome taste!

- pretzels (sounds crazy but Americans love the sweet-and-salty taste and I think they have a point)

- cubes of sponge or Madeira cake

Skewer your fruit, cake or marshmallows, and dip into the hot chocolate sauce. *Bliss!*

Bunting

Skye says . . .

Nothing spells summer at Tanglewood so much as bunting; we used to put it up just for special occasions, but last year Paddy hung the stuff from the treetops in June and we left it there until September. It made every day seem special! And, out of season, Summer and I hang up some of the bunting in our room; it's just too good to pack away for winter. We have tons of bunting that we've bought and made over the years, but it's really easy to make - honest!

YOU WILL NEED:

- scraps of cotton fabric in bright colours and patterns (recycle unwanted clothes, but get permission first!)
- fabric scissors, a needle and thread
- a long length of ribbon or cord
- white glue or a stapler

TO MAKE:

1 Cut the fabric into rectangles so that you can draw a zigzag pattern, as illustrated, to help you cut the triangles. You will have to discard the two pieces to the far left and right, as they are only 'half' triangles.

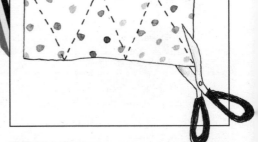

2 Gather your piles of differently coloured and patterned cut-out triangles and choose one.

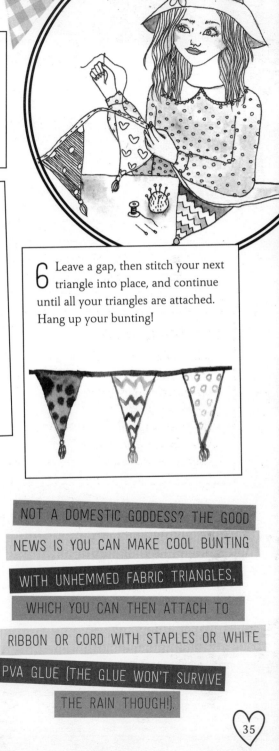

3 Thread a needle. Turn the triangle to the 'wrong' side, and fold back the edges along the sides that slope down to the point of the triangle to make hems. Iron the folds flat if that helps.

4 Stitch the hems down neatly. Hem and neaten all the triangles (you can do this over several days). If you want to be extra cool, add little yarn tassels to the points of each triangle.

6 Leave a gap, then stitch your next triangle into place, and continue until all your triangles are attached. Hang up your bunting!

5 Assemble the bunting. Lay out your triangles in a straight line, 'wrong' side upwards, and varying the colours and patterns as you go along. Lay a piece of ribbon or cord as long as you want the bunting to be across the tops of the triangles. Fold the top edge of the first triangle down over the ribbon or cord and stitch it in place, taking a few stitches through the ribbon to prevent the triangle slipping.

NOT A DOMESTIC GODDESS? THE GOOD NEWS IS YOU CAN MAKE COOL BUNTING WITH UNHEMMED FABRIC TRIANGLES, WHICH YOU CAN THEN ATTACH TO RIBBON OR CORD WITH STAPLES OR WHITE PVA GLUE (THE GLUE WON'T SURVIVE THE RAIN THOUGH!).

**DESIGN SOME
BUNTING FOR . . .**
A BIRTHDAY!
HALLOWEEN!
CHRISTMAS!
EASTER!

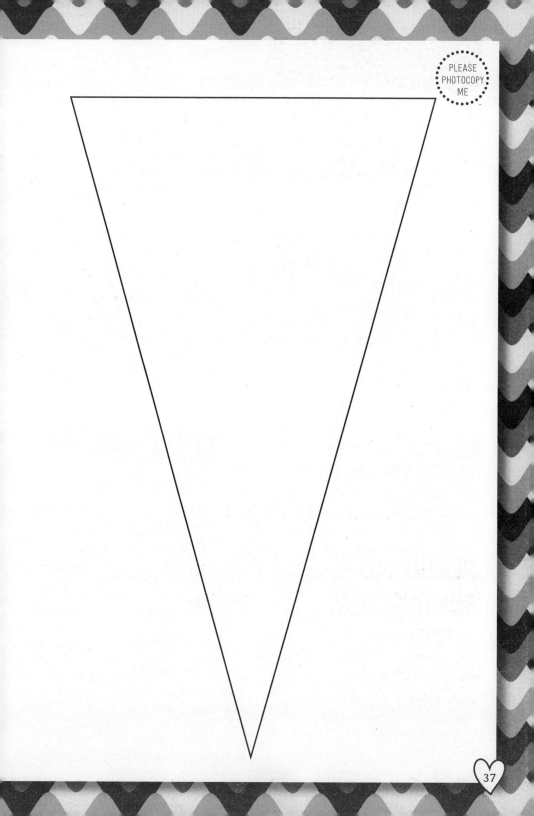

PLEASE
PHOTOCOPY
ME

37

FRUiT ICE LOLLiES

Summer says...

I love baking and preparing food, but most of all I love hunting down recipes for cool sweet treats that are actually good for you! These fruity ice lollies are packed full of flavour and goodness and there's no extra sugar at all — that has to be good, right? They are the perfect way to chill on a hot day.

BEFORE YOU START, MAKE SURE YOU HAVE:

- Ice-lolly moulds (cookshops sell silicone ones cheaply), or paper cups or small plastic beakers (not as pretty, but work well)

- Wooden lolly sticks (cookshops and craft shops stock these; if you're stuck, try a teaspoon frozen into the lolly)

- Access to a freezer with some space

- A selection of juices, yoghurts and other ingredients

STRAWBERRY ICE

YOU WILL NEED:

- 250g fresh strawberries, hulled
- 100ml plain Greek yoghurt
- 1 teaspoon clear honey

METHOD:

1. Blitz the strawberries and yoghurt in a blender.
2. Taste for sweetness and add a teaspoonful of honey if required.
3. Divide the mixture between some lolly moulds or paper cups; add a lolly stick to each one.
4. Freeze until solid (four hours or more).

STRIPY JUICE POPS

YOU WILL NEED:

- 200ml orange juice
- 200ml pink grapefruit juice
- 200ml pineapple juice

METHOD:

1. Pour the orange juice into moulds or paper cups until they are one-third full.

2. Freeze until almost solid, then push a lolly stick into each one (see tip above).

3. Add the pink grapefruit juice until the moulds are two-thirds full; freeze until almost solid.

4. Top with the pineapple juice and freeze until solid.

When putting lolly sticks in, ensure the stick stays in a central position by stretching two strips of sticky tape across the top of the cup, keeping the lolly stick sandwiched between them.

SMOOTHIE OPERATOR

- You can make ice lollies from any of the smoothie recipes on pages 26 and 27.

- Home-made lollies will last for a couple of weeks in the freezer (leave them in the moulds until you want to serve them) but they taste best if eaten the first week after making!

- To release a lolly from its mould, warm the mould or cup with your hands or dip it briefly into warm water.

Feathered Headband

Honey says...

OK, OK, I admit it: I love headbands. Totally. They just make a huge style statement and lift whatever you're wearing; what's not to love? This feathered headband is part festival-chic and part 1920s vintage cool. Plus, feathers are just so pretty. I collect cool feathers whenever I see them, and living in the countryside I find some good ones, but you can also buy them from any good art or craft shop.

YOU WILL NEED:

- feathers large and small; a variety of colours and patterns
- plain cotton fabric to make headband
- fabric scissors
- needle and thread
- elastic or ribbon to fasten
- hot-melt glue gun or white PVA glue
- a vintage brooch or broken earring to decorate

TO MAKE:

1 Cut a piece of fabric to 18 x 18cm and fold it in half. Use the template shown on the next page to draw a curved top on the fabric and cut along the line.

2 Stitch a neat hem round all the fabric edges.

3 Measure one length of elastic or two lengths of ribbon to fit round your head from the ends of the headband, and firmly stitch in place.

4 Open out your fabric as shown and arrange the feathers so you are happy with them. The tallest ones should go in the middle, but otherwise it's up to you.

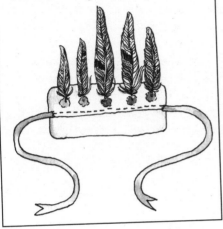

5 Use a hot-melt glue gun, white PVA glue or your needle and thread to secure the bases of the feathers to the headband.

6 Glue an offcut of fabric over the feather bases for strength and to secure the feathers in place.

7 Fold the headband fabric over and stitch neatly to finish it off. Add a vintage brooch or broken earring to the front centre of the headband to complete it. Wear your statement headband and watch the heads turn!

VARIATION

Not brave enough to wear a full-on feather headband? Ease yourself into the look by attaching a few smaller feathers to a hairslide with a hot-melt glue gun. Gorgeous!

Add a cool vintage brooch to your headband

TEMPLATE
100%

PLEASE PHOTOCOPY ME

YOUR SPACE . . .

DESIGN YOUR OWN HEADBAND

A PERFECT PICNIC

COCO SAYS...

I think picnics are amazing all year round, but there's no denying that summer is the best season of all for them. For me, the perfect picnic is an expedition, an adventure — but the food is clearly an important part too! Some of my most memorable meals have been eaten outdoors: squashed sandwiches and a thermos of soup in the ruined cottage on the moors with Lawrie when we rescued the ponies; chip-shop chips on the beach in winter with my sisters; a bar of chocolate in the big oak tree after violin practice — these are just a few! Don't sit around and wait for things to happen; get out there and make some memories. Choose a clear, sunny day, call up some intrepid friends and head for the hills . . .

1 DECIDE ON YOUR MODE OF TRANSPORT

- **BICYCLE** (take a puncture repair kit!)
- **PONY** (I know, I know... but wouldn't it be *awesome*?)
- **TRAIN OR BUS** (find out the time of the last one home)
- **FOOT** (don't plan on trekking ten miles; you'll end up with blisters, or calling home to beg for a lift back!)

2 WHERE WILL YOU GO?

- ask family or friends for advice
- study maps
- discover somewhere new or explore somewhere close by that you've always overlooked
- beside a river or on the beach
- to the countryside or a park
- to an old castle or stately home
- in the city!

3 PICNIC ESSENTIALS

What you take will depend on how you're travelling, but include these:

- ✔ a picnic blanket
- ✔ cups, plates, knives, forks, spoons (brightly coloured and unbreakable if possible)
- ✔ camera or mobile
- ✔ a musical instrument
- ✔ a tea towel, tablecloth or wet wipes
- ✔ a rucksack or wicker basket

4 THE FEAST!

- sandwiches or rolls: cheese and onion, egg mayo, peanut butter and banana — whatever floats your boat!
- cheese, hummus, falafels, crisps
- apples, plums, oranges
- cake — choose your favourite and bring plenty!
- biscuits or flapjacks (beware of chocolate; it will melt on a hot day)
- home-made smoothies or lemonade

5 WHAT TO DO!

- Ask everyone to bring something and, when you get to your destination, settle down, spread the picnic blanket and tablecloth and set out the food; it's more fun if you share.

- Paddle, swim, play rounders, play music, talk, plan, take selfies, dream!

- If you've opted for a winter picnic, choose a sheltered location, dress warmly and bring flasks of soup and hot chocolate.

- If all else fails, a picnic in the park or even the garden can be just as much fun as going somewhere new!

Sunshade Style

Cherry says...

I have to wear sunglasses in bright weather or I get all squinty. I try never to buy expensive sunnies as I can be quite careless and forgetful – I lose a couple of pairs every year! Buying cheap sunnies doesn't mean they have to be dull, though; you can get creative, customize and make them cool and fun – and then imagine you're soaking up the sun in Los Angeles or Barbados!

YOU WILL NEED:

- nail varnish in both clear and bright colours
- glitter
- a hot-melt glue gun or glue spots
- a set of false eyelashes that are extra long and glitzy
- a length of sequin trim

Glitter Shades

TO MAKE:

1 Paint the plastic frame of your sunglasses with bright nail varnish, one part at a time

2 While the nail varnish is still wet, sprinkle on a little pinch of glitter. Have you ever used this trick on your nails? That works, too!

3 Once you've painted and glittered the whole of the frames, allow the varnish to dry. Then add a topcoat of clear varnish to seal.

Flutter Shades

TO MAKE:

1 Take a set of false eyelashes – the crazier the better. Extra-long gold or silver ones look fab!

2 Make sure you have top and bottom lashes for each eye.

3 Glue the lashes along the top of the sunglasses, at the top edge of the lenses just below the frame.

4 The longer top layer of lashes should go towards the outside top edge of the frame.

5 The slightly shorter lower lashes should go towards the inside top edge (overlap or trim to size if you need to).

Sequin Shades

Simply glue a strip of sequin trim along the top of your sunglasses! *Gorgeous!*

47

Your space . . .

PLAN YOUR
PERFECT HOLIDAY

AUGUST

a Brilliant BBQ!

COCO SAYS...

My sisters have given me a bit of stick since I went vegetarian, even though I know they support me really. The whole family eats veggie a lot of the time, but one occasion when meat is bound to feature is when we have a barbecue. I don't object to other people eating meat, obviously — it's a free country — but I wanted to show everyone that you can have an amazing barbie without it. My meat-free barbecue was a big success; so much so that lots of the guests didn't even notice that there wasn't any! Here's what I did.

Set the scene

* Set outdoor tables with pretty cloths. If you think it might get breezy, knot a pebble into the corners of each tablecloth to stop it blowing away.

* Decorate the tables with greenery or bunches of garden flowers in jam jars.

* Bunting (see page 34), fairy lights and jam-jar lanterns (see page 228) are a must.

* Lay the tables with mismatched china and cutlery, and pitchers of home-made cool drinks and smoothies (see page 26).

PREPARE AHEAD

* Big bowls of green salad, coleslaw, hummus, potato salad

* French bread, pitta bread, wholemeal rolls

* Relish, mustard, sauces

Grill on the BBQ

* **QUORN OR VEGGIE SAUSAGES AND BURGERS**

* **SLICES OF HALLOUMI CHEESE:** place on foil and grill; fab with burgers or on their own.

* **VEGGIE KEBABS:** skewer alternate cherry tomatoes, button mushrooms, courgette slices and cubes of feta cheese; drizzle with olive oil and sizzle.

* **STUFFED RED PEPPERS AND FIELD MUSHROOMS:** slice sweet red peppers (the long pointy kind look especially good) and scoop out the seeds; oil the skins of the peppers. Fill with cream cheese, sprinkle with basil leaves and grill on the barbie. This works well with field mushrooms too!

* **CORN ON THE COB:** dot corn cobs with butter, wrap in a double layer of foil, and grill for 30 minutes or until tender and browned.

I got my sisters to help with the food and asked Paddy to organize the barbie. Worrying about whether the charcoal is hot enough is the last thing you need!

SIZZLIN' SWEET TREATS

* GRILLED FRUIT KEBABS: skewer chunks of pineapple, peach, strawberry and banana, and gently brown on the barbie.

* WARM PINEAPPLE RINGS: grill sugar-sprinkled pineapple rings briefly to warm and serve with ice cream.

* BAKED CHOCOLATE BANANAS: slice bananas in their skins lengthwise, being careful not to cut right through. Push chocolate buttons or thin slices of chocolate into the incision, then close the bananas again. Wrap in a double layer of foil and bake in the barbie embers for 15 minutes. Again, great with vanilla ice cream!

Headscarf Suntop

Honey says...

I like fashion, but I try to follow my own style - and I love having something nobody else has! When I was in Sydney I had to change my whole wardrobe to suit the weather; it is so sunny there and I just didn't have enough summery clothes. This is a suntop I made that year from a vintage scarf my sister Skye had given me. It looks great and still gets me lots of compliments even now. Plus it's so easy to make - hardly any sewing at all, promise!

YOU WILL NEED:

- two 30cm lengths of ribbon
- a silky square vintage scarf (charity shops are a great hunting ground — or ask your gran!)
- a needle and thread

TO MAKE:

1 Carefully iron the scarf with the iron on a low setting, and hold it up against you in a diamond shape.

2 Fold the top point over at the level of your collarbone for the neckline; quickly iron the fold.

3 Stitch a 30cm length of ribbon on either side of the folded neckline; these tie the top behind your neck.

4 Try the top on (it's a suntop, so be brave; nothing underneath). Knot the side points behind your back. If the scarf is very small, you can stitch ribbon ties on to the side points too.

GRAB THE SUNTAN CREAM AND GET
OUTSIDE TO CATCH SOME RAYS
IT REALLY IS THAT EASY!

MY SUMMER FASHION IDEAS

SUMMER PUDDING

Cherry says . . .

I am kind of hopeless in the kitchen, but this is a sweet treat I learned to make during my first summer at Tanglewood, and I love it because there is *no baking* involved! It's just a case of assembling the ingredients, and even I can do that! For a really impressive and fruity summer treat, give it a go!

YOU WILL NEED:

- several slices of white or brown bread (from a sliced loaf)
- a small sharp knife
- a large pudding bowl
- 2 or 3 punnets of fresh or frozen summer fruit (raspberries, redcurrants, blackcurrants, blackberries, strawberries)
- sugar or clear honey to taste
- a small saucepan
- a little water
- a saucer or side plate

METHOD:

1. Cut the crusts off the bread and discard. Line the pudding bowl with the crustless slices. Start with a square on the bottom and squares round the sides; cut strips and wedge shapes to fill any gaps so the inside of the bowl is completely covered.

2. Trim and hull the fruit, if it's fresh. Place it in the saucepan with a little water and heat gently until the fruit begins to cook and the juices are released – this should take just a minute or two, or perhaps a little longer if you're using frozen fruit.

If disaster strikes and your pudding doesn't come out perfectly, serve it straight into dishes – it will still taste awesome!

3. Remove the saucepan from the heat when the fruit is soft but still retains its shape. Add a spoonful of sugar or honey and taste for sweetness; add a little more if needed.

4. Drain and reserve some of the juice, setting it to one side. The remaining mixture should be not too wet or too dry.

5. Pour the fruit mixture into the bread-lined bowl until it's full.

6. Place a square of bread over the top of the pudding bowl and add strips of bread if necessary to cover completely; no fruit should be visible.

7. Place a saucer or side plate on top of the pudding bowl and a weight on top to press it down (a tin of beans works well).

8. Place the whole thing in the fridge overnight.

9. To serve, remove the weight and saucer and run a knife carefully round the sides of the bowl to loosen the pudding. Then place a serving plate on top of bowl and turn the whole thing over. The summer pudding should slide out whole.

10. The bread will be soaked and marbled with fruit juice and should look great. Pour the reserved fruit juice over the top as a sauce and serve with ice cream.

Hair Wraps

Skye says...

We've never been on holiday abroad, apart from one time when we visited Grandma Kate in France years ago, but who doesn't love a bit of holiday magic in their summer? Some of my friends have had awesome hair wraps done on holiday, and between us we worked out how to do them for ourselves. These are a lot easier than they look, especially if you have a willing friend or sister to practise on! Here are two of my favourite kinds.

YOU WILL NEED:

- scissors
- embroidery threads in four colours
- hairgrips
- snag-free elastic bands

Simple Hair Wrap

TO MAKE:

1 Cut lengths of embroidery thread in four different colours; the threads should be three times the length of the hair being braided, or a little longer. Take all the strands in your hand and fold them in half, securing the halfway point in the curve of a hairgrip so that the grip is holding the threads and equal lengths hang down on either side.

2 Separate the hank of hair you want to wrap and pin the remaining hair out of the way. Comb the hank and plait it neatly, securing it with an elastic band. Push the hairgrip with its strands of thread into the hair just above or to one side of the plait you have made.

3 Choose a colour to start with and wrap the thread round the plait as tightly as you can, holding the other colours tightly to the plait as you go. Don't rush — hold it firmly and wrap neatly and tightly, covering the hair completely.

4 To change colours, add the starting threads to the other colours and choose a new colour to wrap with; keep your grip firm and don't let go or the whole thing will unravel! Begin your new colour by overlapping it with the last one a few times to make a tight join.

5 Keep going until you near the end of the braid. You can use all the colours to wrap the last few centimetres, which will give you a multi-coloured effect.

6 Secure the end with another 'invisible' elastic. You can add beads or charms to the end of the wrap if you like. This wrap will stay looking good for a few weeks; just hold it out of the way when you wash your hair. To undo, remove the band at the bottom and unwind the threads gently.

Bright Weave

YOU WILL NEED:

- lengths of embroidery thread
- scissors
- an embroidery hoop
- a large-eyed, blunt tapestry needle

TO MAKE:

This is exactly like weaving, so if you've ever done that at school or in a craft club, you are off to a good start.

1 Select a hank of hair: this should be a thin layer about 8cm wide. Gently ease an embroidery hoop over the top part of the hair, being careful not to pull, especially as you snap the hoop closed.

2 Holding the hoop carefully, thread a needle with your chosen colour and take it through the hair in an under/over movement. When you reach the edge of the hank of hair, turn and run the thread back again, moving slowly down.

3 Change colours as you wish and hide the tail ends of the thread underneath the hair. Keep the designs simple and don't weave too tightly; this will take time and care to unpick!

Your space . . .

MAKE A COLLAGE OF YOUR FAVOURITE SUMMER HOLIDAY PHOTOS

Message in a Bottle

Summer says . . .

We spend a lot of our Tanglewood summers on the beach, and a few times over the years my twin and I have sent off a message in a bottle to see if anyone might reply. Once, when we were about eight, we had a letter from a woman in Ireland who had found our bottle washed up on her local beach. That was pretty cool - and Mum says some people have had replies from France, Canada and even India! There's a kind of magic about the ocean, as though it can take your hopes and dreams and carry them into the future. Sometimes I even wonder if it can take your fears and worries and carry them far, far away, where they can't hurt you any more. That's what I was thinking when I threw my pointe shoes into the sea a couple of years ago. Well, maybe a bottle can carry your troubles away too? If you don't live near the ocean, this is one to try on holiday or on a day trip to the seaside.

Is There Anybody There?

YOU WILL NEED:

- a bottle with a screw-top lid or a cork
- white label stickers
- pens, coloured pencils and felt-tip pens
- writing paper
- string or thread
- glitter
- sand, seashells, seaweed, sea-glass – whatever you can find!

1 Take a glass bottle with a screw-top lid, or a cork that fits tightly. Scrub the bottle clean and remove any labels if possible.

2 Design your own new label. It will run and wash off when you put the bottle in the ocean, but drawing it focuses energy and good luck, I think. (I know, I know, call me superstitious if you want; I don't care.)

3 Write your letter. Include your name (or a nickname), the date and the year, but don't give your address or any personal information. Instead write about your hopes, dreams, wishes and thoughts on life.

4 Conclude by asking the finder to keep your letter and to send one of their own; the idea is not to get a reply, but to start a chain of letters in bottles.

5 Roll your letter up, tie it with string or thread and push it into the bottle. Include a pinch of glitter for good luck.

6 Launch your bottle just after the tide has turned, so the waves will carry your bottle far out to sea (if you do it before high tide, the bottle will end up back on the beach at your feet).

63

Send Your Troubles Out to Sea

I love the idea of letting go of your troubles, because there have been a few of those for me over the last year or two. And letting the sea wash our worries away has to be worth a try. I wrote a letter earlier this year, listing some things I wanted to let go of, then put the letter in my bottle and sent it out to sea. In a funny way, I think it helped — I felt lighter and stronger for doing it. I'm not saying doing this will solve your troubles, but it may help you to let go of them and move on!

1 Again, you need a glass bottle with the labels removed. Design a new label and make it as cool and magical as you can.

2 Put a pinch of sand and a few seashells into the bottle, along with a wisp of seaweed and a few nuggets of sea-glass. It will look pretty and maybe, just maybe, add to the magic.

3 Write your worries or troubles on strips of paper, fold them tightly and push them into the bottle. Do *not* screw on a top or put a cork in.

4 Whisper a message into the bottle, allowing yourself to let go of anything sad, difficult or unwanted.

5 Wade into the water just after high tide and throw your bottle as far as you can. The tide will take it out to sea, but, as the bottle isn't watertight, the water will seep inside and pull it down to the seabed, where the salt water will gradually wash your troubles away to nothing.

Your space...

DESIGN YOUR OWN LABELS
Just add a pretty ribbon!

PLEASE
PHOTOCOPY
ME

AUT

UMN

Although I love every season, there is definitely something special about autumn. It's partly because autumn is the start of a new school year, which I can't help loving; but, mostly, it's all about nature. First of all the swallows gather and fly away, then it's fruit-picking time, and then, before you know it, the leaves are turning to red and gold and the days are getting crisp and cold and frosty. I love the change of temperature too — when it's time to slip back into jeans and jumpers and woolly hats, I'm happy! Time for Halloween and Bonfire Night and long rides along the beach on my pony Caramel. Autumn is just brilliant.

My favourite thing to do in autumn? Dead simple: autumn doesn't officially begin for me until I have caught a falling leaf and made a wish on it. And the wish? To save the giant panda and the Siberian tiger and the white rhino and the Amazon rainforest — obviously.

Coco
xx

Back to School

VINTAGE STYLE

Skye says . . .

I know you're not supposed to, but I secretly love that whole 'back to school' thing when September rolls round. You get to see your friends again, you get a fresh start work-wise and you also get to reinvent your style just a little bit. After all, school uniform rules are there to be gently tweaked, right?

UNIFORM SHOPPING

SEARCH charity shops for retro uniform items. I found a striped school tie, and a cool handknitted black cardi.

I may be the only student at Exmoor High to bend the uniform rules so they are actually stricter and more old-fashioned; a sweatshirt and black trousers are just so dull!

MY FAVE FIND was a black felt school blazer with red piping, probably from the 1960s. It *used* to be part of the Exmoor High uniform, so the teachers can't exactly stop me from wearing it!

A black beret looks good too!

MY BASICS ARE:
• White shirt and black pleated skirt – simple supermarket buys.
• Complete the look with black opaque tights, woolly tights or, in summer, white socks.

I'm putting an awesome red leather satchel on my Christmas list, and I've got my eye on a gorgeous retro navy-blue duffel coat with toggles too – the perfect winter uniform!

FISHTAIL PLAIT

My favourite hairstyle for school has to be the fishtail plait. It's a great vintage look and is really easy to do!

1 Make a side parting and brush your hair over to the side; split all of your hair into two equal sections.

2 Take a small length of hair from the outside of one of the sections and bring it over to the inside of the other section.

3 Then take a small length of hair from the other section and bring it across to the inside of the opposite section. Pull tight.

4 Continue taking small pieces from one side to the inside of the other, alternating sides, until you have the routine and the hair is in a neat fishtail pattern.

5 When it's complete, secure the plait with a no-snag elastic band.

Watch a video tutorial of how to make a fishtail plait on CCTV!

71

CHEATS' BANOFFEE PIE

Honey says...

I like baking, but if I'm honest I like fast, easy recipes and show-stopping results. Who wouldn't? This dessert is my fave party piece - I make it whenever we have a family get-together. I also traditionally make it on the day we all go back to school, because it's the perfect cheer-up treat after that first day back is done . . .

YOU WILL NEED:

- 250g digestive biscuits
- a large mixing bowl
- a rolling pin
- 150g butter
- a saucepan
- a non-stick, loose-bottom flan tin
- 1 x 397g tin ready-made caramel
- 2 bananas
- 1 small bar dark chocolate or 1 teaspoon cocoa powder
- 400ml extra-thick double cream (or ordinary double cream, whipped until it forms peaks)

METHOD:

1. Put a couple of the biscuits into a mixing bowl and crush them into fine crumbs using the end of a rolling pin. Slowly add the rest of the biscuits until they are all finely crushed.

2. Melt the butter in the saucepan and pour it on to the biscuits, then stir. Press the mixture firmly into the flan tin, pressing down with the end of a rolling pin or the back of a spoon.

3. Chill the biscuit base in the fridge for an hour.

4. Remove the flan tin from the fridge and spread the caramel on top of the biscuit base, smoothing it with a knife.
5. Slice the bananas into discs and arrange them on top of the caramel.
6. Spread the cream over the bananas.
7. Grate the chocolate over the top to decorate, or sprinkle it with cocoa powder.
8. Chill again before serving.

WRITE ABOUT OR DRAW
THE SWEETEST THINGS
THAT HAVE EVER
HAPPENED TO YOU . . .

Happy Stones

Summer says...

One thing I've learned over the last few years is that, when you're feeling sad, doing something cool for someone else gives you a buzz and lifts your spirits. When I was at my lowest, not many people noticed or understood what I was going through, yet when you feel that way even one small, encouraging word can make all the difference. Since then, I've made a point of trying to be friendly and supportive to others, because you really don't know what might be going on behind the mask; even if someone is smiling on the outside, they could be breaking on the inside the way that I was.

When we were little, my sisters and I used to collect stones and pebbles from the beach and bring them up to the garden to paint; I used that idea to spread some positive, happy thoughts.

YOU WILL NEED:

- smooth stones, not too big and not too small, that fit neatly in the palm of your hand
- acrylic paints and a waterproof black marker pen
- small paintbrushes
- water
- a list of words or phrases that might make someone smile

List of words

Be awesome
Reach for the stars
You're beautiful
You can do it
You're amazing
Smile
Stay strong
Be brave
Believe
Life is magical
Dream big
Shine on
Cool and clever

TO MAKE:

Practise your painting skills until you're steady, then paint the words and phrases on your stones. If you like, add a couple of heart shapes or flowers, but don't worry if you're not arty — the stones look awesome without any extra decoration. If you cannot master writing with a brush, use a permanent marker pen.

SHARING YOUR STONES:

Leave your happy stones in random places: back on the beach, in a play park, outside a shop, in the playground at school, in a garden, at a picnic spot. Thinking up places to leave them is part of the fun. The messages might make people smile or laugh, and, when someone who really needs that message finds it, they might pick up the pebble and put it in their pocket to keep it close.

VARIATION

♥ HAPPY MESSAGES

Write happy messages or phrases on postcards or Post-it notes and place them inside library books, school textbooks, cafe menus, etc.

Job done! ✳

Shay's Scarf

♥ Cherry says... ♥

Money is short, and my boyfriend, Shay, has a birthday coming up. He works outdoors a lot because he helps with his dad's sailing centre, so I'm making him a scarf to keep him warm now that the weather is starting to turn. I'm not an expert at knitting, but our neighbour back in Glasgow, Mrs Mackie, taught me. And this scarf uses knit stitch (garter stitch) all the way through, so it really is simple enough for anyone to try!

YOU WILL NEED:

- 1 pair of size 9mm/00 knitting needles (big and chunky ones)
- 2 balls of chunky yarn in a colour of your choice
- a few strands of yarn in contrasting colours
- a crochet hook (from a wool shop, or ask your gran!)
- scissors

TO MAKE:

1 Cast on twelve stitches. Knit rows until the scarf is the right length or until you run out of yarn — whichever is sooner. I am going for 1.5m long so there's plenty to wrap round! (A scarf big enough for two; now there's a thought!)

2 Allow plenty of time to make the scarf. The last one I made took me three or four weeks, with me knitting a few rows whenever I got a chance. You can't rush these things!

3 Cast off.

4 To make tassels, cut five pieces of yarn twice as long as you want the finished tassels to be. Hold the strands together and fold them in half so there's a loop at one end.

5 Push the crochet hook gently through a gap in the scarf near the edge of one end; use the hook to pull the loop of strands through the gap.

6 Tug the loose ends of the tassel through the loop and pull tight to make a knot.

7 Make more tassels in the same way all along the bottom edge, and then add tassels to the other end too. Alternatively, add pom-poms to the corners of the scarf (check Google for a quick pom-pom turorial) – I'm not sure Shay would like them as much, though!

IF YOU CAN'T KNIT

Getting someone to show you how to cast on, knit garter stitch and cast off is the easiest way to learn; ask a friend or family member to pass on their skills. They'll enjoy helping you and can make sure you have the technique sorted before you try making something. Cool crafts such as knitting and crochet are coming back, so if you know someone who can teach you, make the most of the chance to learn. If all else fails, you can always Google 'casting on', 'knit/garter stitch' and 'casting off' and watch an online tutorial.

A Cosy Night In

Sometimes, my favourite nights of all are nothing to do with parties or picnics or swish social events; they are the nights I spend at home with my family, curled up on the blue velvet sofas in PJs and onesies, chilling out. Sometimes we watch movies and sometimes we go screen-free and dig out the board games — that's always a lot more fun than you might think. And, if you don't have board games, no worries; there are plenty of games you can play for free!

Fave Family Movies

* **Born Free** (my choice – always makes me cry!)

* **Moonrise Kingdom** (my choice again – love it!)

* **Chocolat** (everyone's all-time favourite!)

* **Pretty in Pink** (Mum's fave, but the others love it too – it's a bit slushy for me!)

* **10 Things I Hate About You** and **The Perks of Being a Wallflower** (Honey's faves – we all secretly like them too!)

* **All the Harry Potter movies** (all of us love these!)

* **It's a Wonderful Life** (Grandma Kate has brainwashed us with this cheesy Christmas movie from the dark ages – now we all love it too!)

WHO AM I?

Someone not joining in writes the names of a series of famous people from films, TV, pop, politics, history, etc. on small Post-it notes. This person then takes one Post-it and sticks it to the forehead of a player. The player asks the rest of the group lots of questions (which have to be answered by 'yes' or 'no' only) in order to guess who they are. Keep going until everyone has had a turn.

Fave Board Games

* **Monopoly** (Paddy, Cherry and Summer are surprisingly good at this; the rest of us are dreadful. If there was a prize for *losing* all your money I'd probably win it)

* **Cluedo** (we love this; murder-mystery fun for one and all)

* **Snakes and Ladders, Tiddlywinks, Scrabble, Connect Four** (nice and retro)

* **Buckaroo, Frustration, Mousetrap, Operation, Twister** (brilliant for laughs)

SHOPPING LIST

A simple memory game that can get very silly. One person starts by saying, 'I went to the corner shop and I bought one loaf of bread.' The next in the circle repeats this and adds an item, for example, 'I went to the corner shop and I bought one loaf of bread and two pairs of red, sparkly high-heeled shoes.' Keep going, adding silly or sensible things and repeating each description accurately, until someone gets the list wrong, then make them do a forfeit (like making the hot chocolate).

YOU CAN ALSO TRY VERSIONS OF CHILDHOOD PARTY GAMES SUCH AS MUSICAL CHAIRS, STATUES, MURDER IN THE DARK, HIDE AND SEEK, PIN THE TAIL ON THE DONKEY AND BLIND MAN'S BLUFF – VERY SILLY AND FUN!

CHARADES

The person setting the challenge chooses a book or a film and uses hand signals to show which of these they are thinking of. They then hold up several fingers to indicate the number of words in the title, and act out the words without speaking until someone guesses the answer.

MY TOP TEN FAVOURITE FILMS!

1 ....

2 ....

3 ....

4 ....

5 ....

6 ....

7 ....

8 ....

9 ....

10 ....

Toffee Apples

You will need:

- 6 lolly sticks
- 6 small eating apples
- 200g demerara sugar
- a small saucepan
- 50ml water
- a wooden spoon
- 1 tablespoon balsamic vinegar
- 20g butter
- 2 tablespoons golden syrup
- 1 teaspoon red food colouring (if you like your toffee apples bright)
- a saucer of sugar sprinkles or hundreds and thousands
- an oiled baking tray

Method:

1. Push the lolly sticks into the apples.

2. Place the sugar in a saucepan with 50ml water over a low heat, and stir with the wooden spoon until the sugar dissolves.

3. Add the vinegar, butter, golden syrup and food colouring (if using) to the pan, and stir gently until everything melts.

4. Bring to the boil and simmer for 5–6 minutes, stirring occasionally.

5. Do not leave the pan at any time! Making toffee is a tricky operation, so get an adult to keep an eye on proceedings (better than burning the pan, which is what happened to me the first time I tried this).

6. Test whether the toffee is ready by dropping a little of the mixture into cold water to see if it hardens. If it does, remove the pan from the heat.

7. Dip the apples carefully into the toffee, swirl to coat them and let the excess drip off.

8. Dip the coated apples into sugar sprinkles or hundreds and thousands if desired.

9. Place on the oiled baking tray to cool and set.

Chocolate-coated apples

You will need:

- 6 lolly sticks
- 6 small eating apples
- 200g milk chocolate
- two heatproof bowls
- a small saucepan of water
- 100g white chocolate
- a baking tray

Method:

1. Push the lolly sticks into the apples.

2. Melt the milk chocolate in a bowl set over a pan of simmering water (don't let the water touch the bowl).

3. When the chocolate has melted, dip the apples to coat them. Set them on the tray and place in the fridge to set.

4. Melt the white chocolate in a clean bowl over the pan of simmering water. Remove from the heat.

5. Hold the apples over the bowl. Use a spare lolly stick to drizzle the white chocolate over the milk-chocolate coating. Place apples in the fridge to set.

Write a Ghost Story

Cherry says...

I may not be great at maths or science or IT, but I totally love writing stories. It's my favourite thing ever. I think it's just the way my mind works; I like to people-watch and often I see, hear or imagine things that trigger an idea. That sets me off daydreaming, and sometimes I end up with a story. My friends occasionally say they get stuck for ideas, so I thought I'd share my writing tips with you.

IDEAS

Ideas are around us all the time, but staring at a blank sheet of paper and hoping for inspiration is fatal. If you're struggling, give yourself a theme. Better still, I'll give you one: write a ghost story! Now think all around that theme and see what you can come up with. If you're still stuck, ask 'what if' questions to open up new possibilities.

HOW TO START

Don't get bogged down with pages of description — jump into the story at an exciting bit and go from there. Build the tension and remember to keep things spooky, chilling and mysterious.

THE ENDING

Finishing a story is about more than just tidying up the loose ends; try to save a surprise or a twist in the tail to jolt the reader a little with something unexpected. And, with a ghost story, if you can make the reader shiver a little too, you know you're on to a winner!

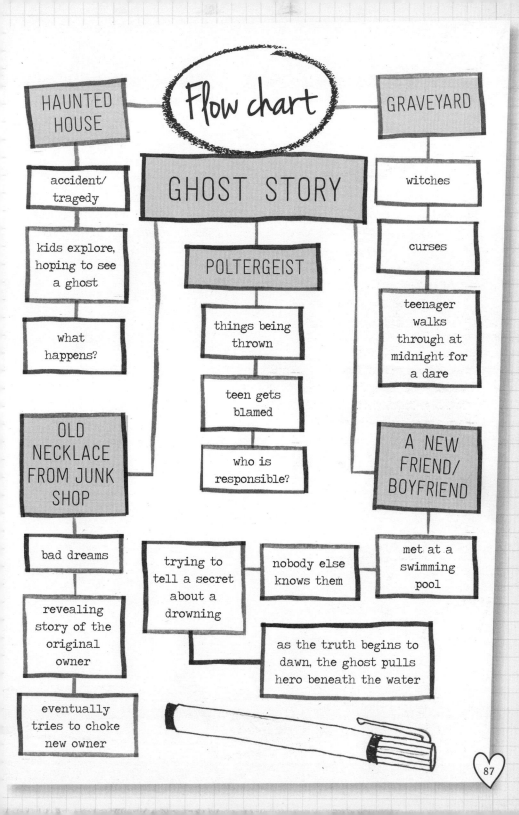

Flow chart

GHOST STORY

HAUNTED HOUSE

accident/ tragedy

kids explore, hoping to see a ghost

what happens?

OLD NECKLACE FROM JUNK SHOP

bad dreams

revealing story of the original owner

eventually tries to choke new owner

POLTERGEIST

things being thrown

teen gets blamed

who is responsible?

trying to tell a secret about a drowning

nobody else knows them

GRAVEYARD

witches

curses

teenager walks through at midnight for a dare

A NEW FRIEND/ BOYFRIEND

met at a swimming pool

as the truth begins to dawn, the ghost pulls hero beneath the water

87

WRITING TIPS

- ✔ Write a little every day, and not just in school time – I write in a journal and often write my own short stories.

- ✔ Write about what you know; it will make your story believable.

- ✔ Make your characters realistic – draw them, scribble notes, think about what makes them tick.

- ✔ Make sure your story has a strong beginning, middle and end.

- ✔ Don't feel you have to write a book-length story; a short story can be the best way to polish up your writing skills.

- ✔ Don't be scared to write in the style of a favourite author. You can learn a lot from doing this (and it won't seem like work at all).

 Your space . . .

WRITE YOUR OWN GHOST STORY

If you love writing, check out the writing comp on WWW.CATHYCASSIDY.COM It's on the Writer's Workshop page in the You section.

Chai, Baby

Honey says...

I first had chai tea in Australia. Ash showed me how to make it, because his family drinks it a lot. Chai is a cross between a smoothie and a sort of tea-latte with a real kick of spices thrown in, and, although in Australia we drank it chilled with ice, my favourite way to have it is hot. Give it a try, and remember, if you don't like the taste at first, you can adapt the recipe and tweak until you're happy.

If someone in your family is curry-mad, you're in luck - you can raid the spice rack! If you don't have exactly the right ingredients, adapt the recipe to what you have - for example, use ground pepper instead of whole peppercorns, ground cinnamon instead of a cinnamon stick, ground ginger instead of fresh. If you're using ground spices, halve the quantities. Treat this like an experiment: add another teabag for a stronger brew, leave out the ginger or cardamon and work out what tastes best to you. Once you have the recipe exactly the way you want it, write it down and guard it with your life! Chai is fab to serve hot at Halloween, Bonfire Night, Christmas, New Year - any wintry celebration, really! And whenever I make it, I think of Ash - that's kind of a bonus, right?

You will need:

- 2 cups water
- a few black peppercorns
- 1 cinnamon stick
- 3 cardamon pods
- 6 whole cloves
- 1 star anise
- 6mm piece of ginger root, finely sliced (or 1 teaspoon lazy ground ginger)
- a saucepan
- 1 Darjeeling teabag
- 2 cups milk
- 3 tablespoons clear honey
- a large jug or pitcher
- pretty cups or glasses

Also try:

❤ **HOT APPLE JUICE:** heat a carton of apple juice with an equal quantity of water, a cinnamon stick, a tablespoon of honey and half a thinly sliced apple.

❤ **MULLED ORANGE JUICE:** heat a carton of orange juice with an equal quantity of water, ½ teaspoon ground ginger, a cinnamon stick, a tablespoon of honey and an orange, sliced and studded with whole cloves.

Method:

1. Put the water, peppercorns, cinnamon, cardamon, cloves, star anise and sliced ginger in a saucepan. Bring to the boil and simmer for five minutes.

2. Remove from the heat. Cover the pan and allow to steep for ten minutes.

3. Add the teabag and bring the mixture back to the boil, then turn down the heat and simmer for another five minutes.

4. Add the milk and heat through until the mixture begins to bubble again. Remove from the heat.

5. Stir in the honey until dissolved. Strain the mixture into a large jug or pitcher and pour into pretty cups or glasses – or, in hot weather, allow the chai to cool and serve it over ice.

Face-paint Crazy

Summer says...

As well as dancing, one of the things I've always enjoyed about being in a stage show is the make-up. Even at the age of five or six, the dance school teachers and their helpers would paint and powder our faces, paint smoky, glittery eyes and slick on bright red lipstick. This has always been part of the whole adventure and thrill for me. By the time I was twelve or thirteen, I was asked to be one of the helpers myself, painting faces and fixing hair in buns for a troupe of five- and six-year-olds. I love it, and I think I'm quite good at it too.

These days I am chief face-painter at home, especially at Halloween. It's a great excuse to go crazy and create a spookily cool look!

YOU WILL NEED:

- a headband
- water-based face paints – ours are from Snazzaroo!
- face glitter
- a beaker and a bowl of water
- small, fine brushes
- make-up sponges
- hairbands or clips
- a towel

IMPORTANT: Check that the person you're painting isn't allergic to the paints. If you're not sure, do a patch test on their arm an hour or two in advance. If there is any redness or itching, no face paint.

TURNED TO STONE

1 Make sure your model's hair is protected by a headband and her clothes are covered by a towel. With white paint, draw a wiggly line as shown from above the model's ear, up across the forehead, down the side of the nose, through the centre of the lips and to below the ear.

2 Dab a clean, damp sponge into white paint and smooth it across the face outside the white line. Take the white paint down across the neck and up to the hairline, covering the mouth, eyelid and eyebrow.

3 Inside the line, make up the face as if for a night out, with blusher, eyeshadow, eyeliner and lipstick.

4 With black paint and a fine brush, go over the wobbly white line and paint little cracks into the white.

SPIDERWEB WITCH

1. Make sure your model is prepared, with hair back and clothing covered. Dab a clean sponge into green paint and smooth it across the face, up to the hairline and down beneath the chin.
2. Paint the lips and eyelids blue, and add glitter to the eye area if you have some.
3. With black paint and a fine brush, paint over each eyebrow, flaring the line up to the temples.
4. Paint a black line and spiderwebs beneath each eye, flaring out across the cheeks. If you like, add a spider!

GHOST EYES

1. With a fine brush, line above and beneath the eyes with black. Go over each eyebrow also and add a shimmer of glitter on the outer edges of the eyes.
2. Paint swirling, spiralling shapes radiating out from the lower eyelids and down across each cheek.

93

Fancy-dress Fun

Skye says . . .

I love dressing up at any time of the year, especially if there's vintage involved! Halloween is special, though, because everyone wants to trick or treat or party. My sisters are always asking me for inspiration and ideas - and ready-made fancy dress outfits, sometimes. They're cheeky like that. I'd love to work in costume design one day, so any excuse to get some practice is fine by me!

YOU WILL NEED:

- black leggings
- a black leotard
- a black T-shirt
- black fur fabric
- a hairband
- a hot-melt glue gun or strong glue
- two pairs of old black tights
- a black top and tights
- a length of elastic
- a couple of black bin bags
- strips of black lace or a shop-bought witch's hat
- face paint
- fake spiders
- old newspapers
- an old white cotton nightdress (a charity shop find)
- red acrylic paint
- an old paintbrush or toothbrush

BLACK CAT

EASY TO DO AND ALWAYS POPULAR!

1. The basic costume is black leggings and a black leotard or long-sleeved top.
2. Make cat ears from fur fabric – two triangles of fabric per ear! Stitch the triangles together, fur-side out, and either glue to a hairband with a hot-melt glue gun or stitch firmly to it.
3. Cut one leg from a pair of old black tights, then chop up the rest of the tights and another pair too, and use them to stuff the leg. Knot the top and stitch to the back of your black leggings to make a tail.

WITCH

1 The basic costume is a black top and tights. Knot a length of elastic round your waist, then slice some bin bags into strips.

2 Knot the strips over the elastic, working your way round to create a rustly bin-bag tutu.

3 Backcomb your hair and tie it up with lots of black lace, or wear a shop-bought witch's hat.

4 Paint your face in the 'Spiderweb Witch' style on page 93.

5 Accessorize with a few fake spiders!

GHOST GIRL

1. Lay out some old newspaper and spread the old white nightdress on top.
2. Mix up red acrylic paint in a paper cup; it should be thick enough to be bright, but runny enough to swish around the cup.
3. Use an old paintbrush or toothbrush to spatter the nightdress with red paint to give the effect of blood. Allow to dry overnight.
4. Match with backcombed hair and the 'Turned to Stone' or 'Ghost Eyes' face-paint designs on page 93.

YOUR SPACE . . . .

DESIGN YOUR PERFECT
HALLOWEEN COSTUME

Bonfire Party

COCO SAYS...

It's not as though we ever need an excuse for a bonfire party at Tanglewood; living by the beach, they're part of every summer. Often we skip the bonfire on November 5th and go to an organized display; we don't do fireworks here at Tanglewood because the animals would hate it, and, besides, big firework displays are always much more dramatic and exciting. I don't think anyone does bonfires better than we do, though, and November seems a good time to tell you how we do them. Here goes!

Prepare:

1. Fire can be dangerous, so get an adult to take charge of lighting and looking after the bonfire.

2. Choose a site well away from the house and any trees, sheds, fences or overhead wires or cables. Warn neighbours before; better still, invite them!

3. Dig a shallow pit to contain the bonfire. Have buckets of sand or water in case you need to douse the flames.

4. Gather dry wood, pine cones, dry leaves, wood shavings and paper.

5. Stack the wood under cover and build the bonfire just before you light it; that way there's no danger of hedgehogs or small animals hibernating inside it.

6. Charcoal briquets are a safe way to start the fire. Never use paraffin or petrol. All fire tending should be done by an adult. Lay briquets in the centre of the pit and surround with scrunched newspaper, dry twigs and tinder. Add larger sticks around these in a little pyramid, and thicker logs once the fire is lit. A metal firepit or a chimenea is a good option in a smaller garden.

7. Arrange chairs, upturned crates or big logs around the bonfire for seating.

DECORATE:

• String fairy lights through trees and along fences, and dot solar-powered lights along pathways.

• Tie up some ultraviolet or glow-in-the-dark balloons in the trees nearby.

Listen to:

✳ Live music! Get friends or family to bring guitars, penny whistles, flutes, djembe drums, mouth organs, etc. I usually offer to play violin, but nobody seems too enthusiastic . . .

✳ If nobody plays an instrument, have a singalong instead.

✳ You could make a playlist and connect your MP3 to an outside or portable sound system.

ALSO SERVE:

• Soup in paper cups

• Baked potatoes (cheat and cook these in the oven to avoid charred or half-baked disasters)

• Hot dogs (yes, you can get veggie ones)

• Hot drinks or home-made smoothies, depending on the season

Make Toasted Marshmallows!

1. Most marshmallows are not veggie (they contain gelatine) so if, like me, you don't eat meat, ask in your local health food store for veggie ones.

2. Find a long stick and sharpen the tip into a point.

3. Skewer your marshmallow and hold it over the embers until it browns and blisters a little, then eat carefully, because it will be melty and very hot inside!

TRY S'MORES!

Possibly the best & most wicked bonfire treat ever . . .

YOU WILL NEED: marshmallows and digestives

METHOD:
1. Toast marshmallows as above, then use a twig to push the hot marshmallow off the toasting stick and on to a chocolate digestive.
2. Sandwich another biscuit on top, chocolate-side down, and gently squash the marshmallow. The hot marshmallow will melt the chocolate - heaven!

Bring:

• glow sticks for after-dark fun
• sparklers

PLAN A BONFIRE PARTY

* WHO TO INVITE?
* WHAT TO EAT?
* PLAYLIST?
* WHAT TO DO?

Leaf Messages

Cherry says . . .

We were asked at school to write poems inspired by autumn and then decorate them in an autumny way. It was a fab project because it got everyone thinking about the way the seasons change.

I had the idea of writing my autumn poem on an actual leaf, but fallen leaves are quite brittle so it didn't really work - until Charlotte told me this trick to preserve them! It's really easy, and when the leaves were done I wrote my poem on them in black marker pen. I still had lots left over, and that's when my stepsisters decided to get in on the act and the whole thing turned into something else completely. I think my stepsisters are seriously cool; I really do!

YOU WILL NEED:

- a bottle of glycerine (from a chemist; glycerine is a sugar compound, non-toxic and used in moisturizers and cosmetics — nothing scary, honest!)
- a wide, shallow dish and a smaller plastic dish
- a selection of large, dry, clean fallen leaves (go for a walk in the country or a park to gather different varieties)
- kitchen paper
- a waterproof black marker pen with a slim nib
- a needle and some cotton embroidery thread
- scissors
- a small hammer
- panel pins

TO MAKE:

1 Pour the glycerine into the large, wide dish. Use the empty glycerine bottle to add two bottles of water to the dish, giving you one part glycerine to two parts water. Stir the mixture.

2 Place the leaves in the dish and push them gently so they are submerged. You can layer the leaves, one on top of the other, as long as each is placed in individually and thoroughly coated with the solution.

3 Place the smaller plastic dish on top of the leaves to keep them submerged, and place the dish in a safe place for a week or two.

4 Remove the leaves and blot them dry with kitchen paper. They should be glossy and pliable.

LEAF QUOTES AND MESSAGES CAN BE FIXED TO TREES, GATES, WOODEN POSTS AND WOODEN FRAMES USING A SINGLE PANEL PIN.

NEXT . . .

5. Collect autumn poems and haikus – or write some of your own! Look up autumn-inspired or uplifting quotes!

6. Write your poems, quotes and messages on the leaves in marker pen.

7. Link leaves together into a garland with cotton embroidery thread, using a needle and a few knots to space the leaves properly.

8. Find a plain fence or wooden wall to brighten up with a leaf poem (choose somewhere your leaves will be seen but that doesn't involve any trespassing).

9. With a couple of friends or sisters, sneak out early one morning and use the hammer and panel pins to hang the leaf garland – a bit of sneaky art and inspiration!

10. Later, watch people's reactions as they see the leaf messages and poems – but shh! Don't let on that it was you!

Revamp Old Ballet Flats

Summer says...

Ballet flats are my absolute favourite shoes; there was a time when I'd have been happy to wear pointe shoes all day long if I could, but obviously that wouldn't have been practical! Ballet flats are the next best thing; they're the everyday version of proper ballet shoes, aren't they? They make everything look neat and pretty, but although they're cheap and go with just about everything they can get a bit dull after a while. With help from Skye, I've worked out a few ways to liven my old pairs up; who says shoes have to be boring?

Ribbon Ties

YOU WILL NEED:

- ½ metre of wide satin ribbon in a colour that matches your shoes
- sharp scissors
- hot-melt glue gun or strong glue

TO MAKE:

1 Cut the ribbon into two ¼ metre lengths, finishing both ends with a neatly slanting cut to stop them fraying. Find the centre point of one of the ribbon lengths.

2 On the inside sole of one shoe, just in front of where your heel sits, apply glue and press down the centre part of the ribbon. Apply more glue and firmly stick the ribbon to the inner sole and sides of the shoe, allowing the ends to fall over the sides.

3 Do the same with other shoe and other ribbon. When totally dry, slip on your shoes and tie the ribbons in a cute bow.

★ Glitz & Glam

YOU WILL NEED:

- self-adhesive craft gems in a few shapes and colours

TO MAKE:

Do a few sketches to help you decide how to arrange your gems. Once you're happy, stick the gems on to the front upper of one shoe, then work on the other to make sure the pattern is mirrored exactly.

★ Flower Power

YOU WILL NEED:

- hot-melt glue gun or strong glue
- two fake flowers (I used big daisies!)

TO MAKE:

Glue the daisies on to the front uppers in a central position — super easy!

VARIATIONS

♥ Try covering plain pumps with strips of nylon lace trim.

♥ Glue a sequin trim all round the top edges of the shoes.

105

MY DREAM WINTER BOOTS OR SHOES

Winter Wonder Tree

Skye says . . .

The trees look so sad and stark when they lose all their leaves; this is the perfect time of year to turn one of them into a magical wishing tree and liven up a dull wintry landscape, too! Summer, Cherry, Coco and I worked on this project together, and Honey helped us make the heart and star decorations. We picked out a small, twiggy tree in the corner of the playpark in Kitnor and gave it a sparkly makeover about this time last year. It helps if the tree is quite small - you don't want to be balancing on ladders to do your decorating. Keep it simple, and choose a quiet time of day. We worked quickly and the tree wasn't visible from the road, so nobody actually saw us do it - sneaky, huh?

BEFORE YOU START, COLLECT TOGETHER:

* 2 or 3 brightly patterned knitted scarves (look in charity shops or rescue from the back of wardrobes)
* a needle, thread and scissors
* silver or glittery yarn
* pom-poms of various sizes and in bright Christmas colours, ready-threaded on loops for hanging (Google how to make a pom-pom; it's easy peasy)
* acetate, foil and tissue-paper stars and hearts (see below)

Stars and Hearts

YOU WILL NEED:

* sheets of acetate (from an art or craft shop)
* scissors
* sheets of tissue paper in various colours
* white PVA glue and glue spreader
* scraps of coloured foil (sweet wrappers are ideal)
* glitter
* thin nylon cord to make hanging loops

TO MAKE:

1 Trace the star and heart templates on the next page on to acetate and cut out lots of them.

2 Tear tissue paper into small pieces and glue them on to the acetate until the sheets are all covered in a multi-coloured patchwork of tissue paper; add tiny pieces of coloured foil.

3 Use the glue spreader to coat the top of the tissue paper with a thin layer of PVA glue then sprinkle it with glitter.

4 When the glue is totally dry, pierce a hole at the top of each shape and thread cord through to make hanging loops.

DECORATE YOUR TREE

1. Work with a group of friends, for safety and for fun!

2. Go to your chosen tree; one of the group should keep watch while the others work (this is top secret, y'know!).

3. Wrap the knitted scarves tightly round the trunk of the tree, working from the bottom upwards — where one edge meets another, rapidly stitch the edges together until the trunk is covered. This is why you need several people: some to hold, some to stitch.

4. Tightly wrap lengths of silver or glittery yarn round the branches of the tree.

5. Hang pom-poms and your tissue and acetate stars and hearts from the branches.

Sneak away – and keep quiet!

STAR AND HEART
TEMPLATES

100%

PLEASE
PHOTOCOPY
ME

MY DEEPEST SECRETS

Advent Calender

3

An advent calendar is an essential for December, right? When you're little, it has to be chocolate, but now Mum and Paddy run a chocolate business so chocolate isn't as rare or exciting as it used to be! Recently, we came up with an idea for a different kind of advent calendar and it's so easy to make.

YOU WILL NEED:

- 24 small squares of brown paper (approx 6 x 6cm)
- scissors
- a fine paintbrush
- white and black paint
- 24 multi-coloured envelopes
- a glue stick
- white PVA glue and glitter
- 2 nets chocolate coins (optional)
- squares of coloured paper
- fineliner pens
- several metres of bright or striped cord
- 24 wooden clothes pegs

TO MAKE:

1 Cut out the brown paper squares. Using the fine brush, paint the numbers from 1–24 on the squares, alternating white and black paint. Allow to dry.

2 Set out the coloured envelopes in an order that pleases you. Use the glue stick to stick the number squares on to the envelope fronts.

3 Spread a thin layer of white PVA glue randomly on the envelope fronts and sprinkle glitter over them.

4 If you want to include a little bit of chocolate, slip a chocolate coin into each envelope.

5 Now it's just a case of what to write on those squares of coloured paper!

CHRISTMAS MESSAGES OR CHALLENGES

* Make hot chocolate for the whole family
* Watch a Christmas movie
* Bake some Christmas cookies or mince pies
* Play your fave Christmas songs
* Donate toys to a Christmas charity
* Wrap presents
* Go to a nativity play
* Find some family photo memories from the previous year and ask: where were we and what happened just after this photo was taken?

TO ASSEMBLE:

1. Put the challenges, memories or mini prezzies into the envelopes (see the lists below and to the left for ideas!).
2. Pin a length of cord across a wall or the mantlepiece.
3. Peg the envelopes to the cord. All done!

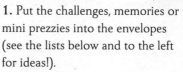

MINI PREZZIES

* lip balm
* nail varnish
* earrings
* key ring
* glow stick
* bookmark
* mini notebook
* fake tattoos
* cool pen
* candy cane
* hairclip
* bracelet
* Christmas decoration
* badge
* stickers

WIN

TER

This is one thing that Summer and I are in total agreement on . . . our favourite season of all is winter. It's not that we don't like spring, summer or autumn – we do. It's just that winter is the most magical. Snuggling up by the fire to watch a movie while Paddy makes toast over the open flames and my sisters lounge about in PJs and outsize jumpers . . . it's my idea of heaven. And don't even get me started on Christmas.

Skye

Summer says...

Winter is definitely the most romantic time of year —
bleak and sad and beautiful. It doesn't snow often at
Tanglewood but, when it does, the world turns white
and everything is SO perfect; it's like life has given
you a clean sheet and anything at all is possible.
Sometimes you think that the world has stopped,
frozen to death, but, no matter how hard the winter
might be, you know that spring will always come. For
me, it's all about new starts, new chances. OK . . . and
Christmas! I rest my case.

Summer ♡

CHRISTMAS: THE RULES

Summer says...

♥ ♡

There's just so much to love about Christmas – and I know I am biased, but Christmas at Tanglewood is the best. We have our own traditions that have evolved over the years. I've written some of them down for you.

1

MAKING THE CHRISTMAS CAKE

Mum starts making the cake on December 1st every year, and we always know when she's doing it because the whole house smells of Christmas! We all have to take a turn stirring it and we get to make a wish as we stir. These days we have chocolate yule log instead of Christmas pudding; Mum hides the old silver sixpence that used to go in the pudding in the cake instead. The sixpence has been handed down from when Grandma Kate was little and whoever gets it in their slice on Christmas Day is supposed to be lucky for the whole year ahead. Except for the time Coco almost broke a tooth on it; some traditions are a little scary!

2 DECORATING THE TREE

We put our tree up on the second Saturday of December. It's always a real one these days. Paddy brings it home strapped to the roof of his little van and it stands in the window of the living room. We have a huge box of decorations in the attic; things we've made over the years and heirloom pieces from when Mum was little. We play Christmas songs, untangle the fairy lights and we all dress the tree together; it's one of the best days of the year.

3 WRITING CHRISTMAS LISTS

This is something we've done ever since we were little, and we still stick to the tradition. We write our Christmas lists on a small piece of paper, usually in mid-December, in the evening with a big open fire roaring away. Sometimes we toast marshmallows too, and Mum brings us hot chocolate as we write. I realize now that this is so she gets to see what we've written! We fold our lists and throw them into the fire – and hopefully they fly up the chimney! Legend has it that if the lists fly upwards we will be lucky at Christmas and get the prezzies we've asked for. Mum usually hovers in the doorway at this point and I think the draught makes the papers fly up above the flames – or maybe it's just magic; who knows? ;o)

1. Snuggly socks
2. Books
3. Charm bracelet
4. Peace

4
CAROL SINGING

Grandma Kate told us that kids went carol singing a lot when she was little, so we decided to revive the tradition. We made a list of our favourite carols, dressed up warm, carried lanterns and went singing from door to door. Shay played guitar and Coco played violin; we had a great time and collected almost £40 for one of Coco's animal charities. A whole new tradition, I think!

CHRISTMAS CAROLS

✓ Away in a Manger
✓ O Little Town of Bethlehem
✓ The Holly and the Ivy
✓ While Shepherds Watched Their Flocks
✓ Little Donkey
✓ In the Bleak Midwinter
✓ Once in Royal David's City

This means that Christmas has finally arrived! Sometimes we make the pastry from scratch (it's easy) and sometimes we cheat with ready-made stuff from the supermarket, plus ready-made mincemeat. We use cutters with a wiggly edge to cut out the pie shapes and a smaller cutter for the lids; but two glasses with different diameters will do! Don't over-fill the pies, or the mincemeat will bubble over and burn. For an extra treat, we sometimes bake the pies without a lid and drizzle home-made icing on top once they've cooled.

5 MAKING THE MINCE PIES

6 HANGING THE STOCKINGS

On Christmas Eve we go to church for a local carol service or a nativity play, which reminds us of the true meaning of Christmas. Then we hang our stockings along the mantlepiece. I bet some of my friends at school would laugh, but who cares? It's what we have always done, and those silly stocking prezzies are one of the best things about Christmas morning! We even leave a mince pie, a truffle and a glass of whisky out for Santa (perks for Paddy, I think).

7 CHRISTMAS MORNING

We still get up stupidly early and open our stockings in our PJs — and every year Paddy is up before us and has the fire roaring away. We get dressed, have breakfast and open our big presents, then it's all hands to work in the kitchen, with Skype calls to Dad and Grandma Kate too. After dinner, we go for a long walk along the beach with Fred the dog and Humbug the sheep, and then it's back home to chill in front of Christmas TV.

123

MY CHRISTMAS WISH LIST . . .

1 ....

2 ....

3 ....

4 ....

5 ....

124

6 ....

7 ....

8 ....

9 ....

10 ....

Tree Fairy

CHARLOTTE SAYS...

I made this tree fairy a few years ago when the girls were small. I wanted something special for our Christmas tree, and although I was run off my feet at the time, looking after four little girls, I also wanted to get creative again. The fairy is made from papier mâché, handpainted with yarn hair and dressed in vintage fabrics. She takes a little time and effort, but I think she's worth it! The girls really love her, so I have a feeling she'll be an heirloom piece.

YOU WILL NEED:

- newspaper (the large kind, ideally)
- masking tape
- cellulose paste (from a craft or art shop) or wallpaper paste (this contains fungicide so keep it away from small children and animals)
- acrylic paints and varnish
- thick and fine paintbrushes
- yarn for hair
- white PVA glue
- a needle and thread
- scraps of netting
- iridescent cellophane
- vintage lace, silk, muslin and ribbon

TO MAKE THE FRAME

1 Spread out a large sheet of newspaper. Begin in one corner and roll the newspaper tightly on a diagonal to make a long, thin, tight paper tube. Secure with masking tape.

2 Fold the paper tube in half. Keep the fold at the top; the neck and body are formed by the top half and the lower part forms the legs. Secure with masking tape.

3 Scrunch up a few small bits of newspaper and place them round the top of your folded tube to make a head. Tweak and tease the paper into shape; use masking tape to hold it in place.

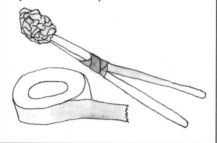

4 Make a smaller paper tube and secure it with masking tape. Fold it in half to form the arms; place the fold just beneath the neck of your fairy frame and attach it with masking tape criss-crossed several times. Trim the arms to the desired length. Tape a few layers of newspaper round the body to thicken it slightly.

TO MAKE THE PAPIER MÂCHÉ

1. Mix a little paste with warm water in a bowl and stir until smooth; aim for the consistency of thick cream.

2. Tear some newspaper into long, thin strips. You will find that the newspaper tears much more easily and evenly in one direction, so always tear this way.

3. Lay strips of newspaper on the surface of the paste. Use your fingers to remove any excess glue and begin wrapping the strips tightly round the head. Cover the head and neck area with three or four layers of papier mâché.

4. Move down the body, aiming for three layers over the whole frame. You can use a brush, but fingers are best for a smooth finish. Be extra neat with the ends of the legs and arms.

5. Set aside to dry thoroughly in a warm place for a day or two.

TO PAINT AND DRESS:

1 Mix a skin colour from acrylic paints — enough to paint the head and body down to the tops of the legs. Allow it to dry, then paint on a second coat, until no trace of the newsprint is visible.

2 Paint the face. Keep it simple, with a red rosebud mouth and black dots for the eyes and nose. Red cheeks are optional.

3 Paint the legs with stripes or spots to make fab stockings. Paint on ballet shoes.

4 When it's completely dry, paint or spray on acrylic varnish for a shiny finish.

5 Cut some lengths of yarn. Spread white PVA glue over the top and back of the head, and lay the strands of yarn over it. Snip the ends so they are even. Add a ribbon headband.

6 Run a series of stitches round the top of some underskirt fabric (I used an old silk scarf). Gather them tightly to fit the fairy's waist and stitch or glue it in place. Drape an overskirt (I used lace and embroidery) over the top, gathering and stitching the fabric in place.

7 Make a bodice from a scrap of lace, stitching it tightly to the fairy.

8 For the wings, lay a rectangle of iridescent cellophane on a rectangle of netting, tying it at the centre to secure. Glue or stitch the wings to the back of the body, or tie them on using ribbon.

9 Tie a ribbon waistband round the fairy and make a loop to hang it at the top of the tree.

YOUR SPACE . . .

DESIGN YOUR PERFECT TREE FAIRY

Felted Christmas Stocking

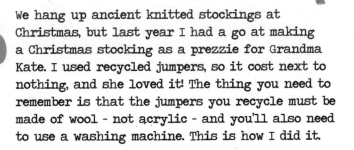

Skye says . . .

We hang up ancient knitted stockings at Christmas, but last year I had a go at making a Christmas stocking as a prezzie for Grandma Kate. I used recycled jumpers, so it cost next to nothing, and she loved it! The thing you need to remember is that the jumpers you recycle must be made of wool - not acrylic - and you'll also need to use a washing machine. This is how I did it.

YOU WILL NEED:

- 2 old wool jumpers (1 cream, beige or a pastel shade and 1 red)
- tracing paper and a pencil
- scissors
- a needle and thread
- Christmassy ribbon or braid in a contrasting colour
- silver star sprinkles
- silver embroidery thread

TO MAKE:

1 First, felt your wool jumpers. Put them in a washing machine set to a hot (90°) wash. The jumpers should come out slightly shrunken, with a thick and dense texture like felt. This won't happen with jumpers made from acrylic or other man-made fibres, so it's important to check beforehand. Some jumpers labelled 'lambswool' are treated against shrinkage and may not felt either, so avoid them. Alternatively you can use shop-bought felt if you prefer, or fleece fabric; neither fray, so they are ideal.

YOU CAN USE FELTED WOOL TO MAKE LOTS OF THINGS LIKE PETAL SHAPES TO MAKE A FELT FLOWER BROOCH; IT'S EASY TO STITCH AND DOESN'T FRAY.

2 Trace round a Christmas stocking on to tracing paper, or use a thick sock as a guide and draw your own pattern. Make the shape chunky — no pointy toes or nipped-in ankles — as it will have to hold prezzies.

3 Pin your pattern to the cream or pastel felted jumper and cut out two stocking shapes.

4 Pin the two stocking shapes together and stitch them together neatly with blanket stitch.

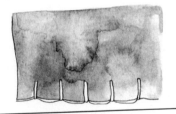

5 Cut a strip of red felt and snip a fringe into one side of it. Using red thread, stitch round the top of the stocking.

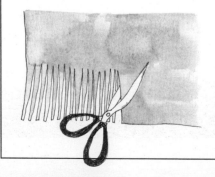

6 Trace the heart pattern template on page 110 and cut it out from red felt; stitch it to the front of the stocking carefully.

7 Stitch the ribbon or braid round the red border, just above the fringing; make a hanging loop to the side. Using fine sewing thread, attach silver star sprinkles with two or three stitches.

8 Decorate the front of the stocking. Stitch on criss-cross stars of different sizes, using silver embroidery thread, then stitch the recipient's name on.

MORE IDEAS:

- heart-shaped tree decorations
- bird-shaped decorations
- a felted-wool headband

131

WHAT I'D LOVE FOR CHRISTMAS

Shoestring Prezzies

COCO SAYS...

I have no idea how people manage to be so organized and save their money up to buy fancy Christmas presents. I never have a penny at Christmas — there are too many good causes I want to support, and those charities need my cash more than I do! I still manage to sort out some cool Christmas presents — all on a shoestring. Making prezzies doesn't mean you're a cheapskate — it means you're putting time and effort into the gift, and not just money. Oh, and it's lots of fun too!

Button Hairclips

YOU WILL NEED:

- old buttons
- scraps of wadding and fabric
- a needle and thread
- a packet of hairgrips
- a hot-melt glue gun or strong glue

TO MAKE:

1 Cover a medium-sized button with a small scrap of wadding and a larger square of fabric; pull the fabric tight behind the button and sew a couple of stitches to secure it.

2 Slide a hairgrip down through the back of the stitched fabric; a spot of hot glue will keep it in place. Alternatively, stitch it on securely.

3 Add a ribbon bow behind the button for a pretty twist.

How to cover your button

134

Hot Chocolate Mix

OK, so it's not quite as awesome as Honey's recipe on page 160 but it still tastes fab, and looks amazing too! It'll keep for two weeks in a sealed jar so make it just before you gift it.

YOU WILL NEED:

- a beautiful home-made label (let your creativity go wild)
- a clean jam jar with the labels scrubbed off
- a grater
- 125g dark chocolate
- 40g caster sugar
- 30g cocoa powder
- a parcel label and curling ribbon

TO MAKE:

1 Stick your label on to a jam jar. Experiment with brown or black paper with 'Hot Chocolate' painted or collaged on.

2 Coarsely grate the dark chocolate. Mix the caster sugar and cocoa powder together, straight into the jar, and stir in the grated chocolate (or layer each ingredient separately for a striped effect).

3 Screw the lid on tightly.

4 Write instructions for making the hot chocolate on a parcel label: 'Place a heaped table-spoon of hot chocolate mix in a mug and top with hot milk or a mixture of milk and boiling water. Stir and serve!'

5 Tie the label round the neck of the jar and store it in the fridge until you're ready to gift it.

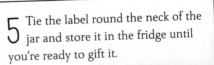

135

Bath Fizz Bombs

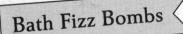

YOU WILL NEED:

- ½ cup bicarbonate of soda
- 1/6 cup cream of tartar
  (supermarket baking section)
- two bowls
- 1 teaspoon olive oil
- 5 drops of essential oil – try
  orange, vanilla or lavender
  (from health food shops)
- a few drops of food colouring
- a bath-bomb mould or silicone
  muffin case
- cellophane
- curling ribbon

TO MAKE:

1 Sift the bicarbonate of soda and cream of tartar together in a bowl and mix well.

2 Mix the olive oil, essential oil and food colouring in a second bowl. Pour them into the powder bowl and mix very quickly with your fingers. Be fast, or the fizz reaction may begin.

3 The mixture will be powdery, but will clump together when squeezed. Press it into the mould, packing the mixture tightly, and leave it to dry for 24 hours.

4 Remove the bomb from the mould, wrap it in cellophane and tie a ribbon round it.

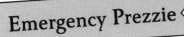

I AM SENDING PRESENTS TO . . .

Emergency Prezzie

YOU WILL NEED:

- a square of coloured netting fabric
- a square of iridescent cellophane
- individually wrapped sweets
- curling ribbon, fabric ribbon or raffia

TO MAKE:

1 Lay the netting on a flat surface and put the cellophane square on top.

2 Place five or six sweets in the centre, gather the net and cellophane up around them and tie with ribbon.

137

CHRISTMAS CRACKERS

Cherry says... ♥

The tradition of making crackers is one Dad and I brought to Tanglewood. It started years ago, when Dad forgot to buy crackers and didn't realize until Christmas Day. He felt awful, so I made a couple using cardboard loo-roll middles, wrapping paper and my own cheesy jokes, with a whole load of sweets inside as the present. They were cool, and we began to do home-made crackers every year. Now, with a bit of input from my arty stepsisters, the crackers are even better - and the gifts you put inside can be personalized for each individual. They're a great way of making a little prezzie for a friend look extra special too!

YOU WILL NEED:

- cracker snaps (from a craft shop)
- cardboard loo-roll middles
- silver star sprinkles
- home-made Christmas jokes
- small gifts
- scissors
- bright patterned paper, a little thicker than regular Christmas wrap; or brown paper, for a vintage look
- a glue stick
- bright or metallic curling ribbon, raffia (from craft shops) or satin ribbon
- small tie-on parcel labels

TO MAKE:

1 Thread a cracker snap through the middle of a loo-roll cylinder and put a small wrapped present in the cylinder. Add a pinch of star sprinkles, a home-made Christmas joke and a small gift.

2 Cut a rectangle of paper just big enough to roll round the loo-roll cylinder and overlap a little so it sticks out 8cm or so on either side.

3 Lightly stick the paper to the cardboard cylinder with the glue stick; add a line of glue along the edge of the paper to make it into a tube.

4 Lay a length of raffia or ribbon under the paper tube at either end of the loo-roll middle. Adjust the cracker snap and make sure everything is even and in place.

5 Gently tie the ribbons into bows, gathering in the paper tube. Use your fingers to neaten the shape.

6 If you're using curling ribbon, draw a scissor blade carefully along the trailing ends of ribbon to make it curl. If you have raffia, use your fingers to split and fray the ends.

COOL CRACKER GIFTS

* tiny hand mirror
* hairclips
* vintage brooch
* bandana
* mini playing cards
* mini sparklers

CHRISTMAS JOKES

Q: WHAT SORT OF PIZZA DOES GOOD KING WENCESLAS LIKE?

A: DEEP PAN, CRISP AND EVEN.

Q: What did Santa say to Mrs Claus when he looked out of the window?

A: Looks like reindeer!

Q: WHAT DO YOU CALL A PERSON WHO IS SCARED OF FATHER CHRISTMAS?

A: CLAUSTROPHOBIC.

Chocolate Truffles

PADDY SAYS...

Things have changed a lot since the days when I started experimenting with truffle recipes in the kitchen of our old flat in Glasgow but, even though I run a chocolate business of my own now, those early truffles take some beating! Here's a recipe that's always popular at this time of year — and it makes lots, so you can eat some and give some away as presents.

You will need:

Makes about 60 truffles

- 340g good quality chocolate
- mixing bowl
- 60g softened butter
- 200ml double cream
- 50g caster sugar
- 2 tablespoons cocoa powder
- a saucepan
- 2 tablespoons icing sugar

Method:

1. Break up the chocolate. Chop it finely and place it in a mixing bowl with the softened butter.
2. Place the cream and caster sugar in a saucepan. Bring to the boil, then remove from the heat.

3. Pour the cream mixture over the chocolate and butter, and beat until all the chocolate has melted and the mixture is smooth and shiny.

4. Freeze for a few hours, until the mixture is firm enough to shape.

5. Mix the cocoa and icing sugar together. Dust your hands with this and roll the chocolate mixture into truffle shapes.

6. Keep in an airtight container in the fridge for up to a week.

The Chocolate Box

You will need:

- white PVA glue
- scissors
- a selection of old magazines and catalogues to cut up
- a small cardboard box with a lid
- tissue paper
- tiny truffle cases
- ribbon

To make:

1. Using white PVA glue, stick pics from magazines of chocolates, flowers, cakes or Christmas motifs on the outside of the cardboard box, découpage style. Brush white PVA glue over the top of the finished découpage – it will be shiny when dry, like varnish, and help to protect the design.

2. Leave the box to dry thoroughly.

3. Line the box with a folded sheet of tissue paper.

4. Place the truffles in paper cases and put them into the box.

5. Put on the lid and tie it up with a ribbon.

141

It's a Wrap . . .

Honey says...

My favourite bit of Christmas is always wrapping the prezzies; it just seems to sum up all the excitement and magic. Wrapping presents is a kind of art form in itself, and if you keep it simple, the results can be stunning. Want to make a real style statement with your gift wrap? Here's how.

Natural Vintage

YOU WILL NEED:

- a roll of brown paper
- sticky tape, a glue stick and a hot-melt glue gun
- scissors
- scraps of cotton, muslin, hessian or lace
- rough string, cord or raffia
- feathers, fir cones or evergreen branches

HOW TO WRAP:

1. Wrap the prezzies in brown paper and use a little tape to secure.

2. Cut muslin, hessian or vintage cotton fabric into wide ribbon bands and pull at the fibres on the long edges to fray them. Wrap the bands round the parcel and use a glue stick or a hot-melt glue gun to keep them in place.

3. Criss-cross the wrapped prezzie with rough string, cord or raffia, and tie in a bow.

4. Tuck a feather or a sprig of evergreen behind the string or raffia, or tie on some fir cones.

Snowflake Wrap

YOU WILL NEED:

- royal blue or crimson tissue paper
- sticky tape or a glue stick
- scissors
- white typing paper or paper doilies
- white ribbon, cord or raffia

HOW TO WRAP:

1 Wrap your prezzies in the tissue paper and secure with a little tape.

2 Make paper snowflakes. Cut white paper into squares of varying sizes. Fold the squares in half to make triangles, then in half again to make smaller ones . . . fold them a third time if you can.

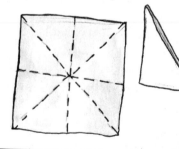

3 Hold the centre point of the snowflake and snip triangles, circles and curving shapes out of the folded edges; snip into the central point too. Unfold your snowflake. Make lots; you will get better and more adventurous as you go! You can look online for tutorials on how to make more intricate snowflake shapes.

4 Use a glue stick to neatly stick the snowflakes on to the tissue paper – or cheat and use paper doilies instead!

5 Tie up with white ribbon or raffia.

White and Gold

YOU WILL NEED:

- white and gold tissue paper
- sticky tape
- scissors
- gold foil (sweet wrappers are good)
- a glue stick
- gold raffia (from a craft shop) or gold cord or ribbon
- thread
- little gold bells (From a craft shop)

HOW TO WRAP:

1 Wrap the prezzie in white tissue paper and secure it with a little tape.

2 Tear gold tissue paper into small squares. Don't be too precise – the torn edges are part of the appeal. Snip gold foil into smaller random shapes.

3 Use a glue stick to stick gold tissue patches on to the white tissue-wrapped prezzie. Add random gold foil shapes on top.

4 Wrap with gold raffia or ribbon and tie in a bow.

5 Thread a couple of small gold bells on a length of thread and tie on to the raffia or ribbon.

Your space . . .

DESIGN YOUR OWN
WRAPPING PAPER

New Year, New Me!

Summer says... ♡

January 1st. Ooh, it's the first day of a brand-new year and the best possible time for a new start — for being the very best version of you it is possible to be. I love January 1st because it feels like you're looking out on a field of newly fallen snow. Nothing has spoilt and it is still perfect. The year ahead is like that too, and I always feel full of hope that this will be the year I finally get on top of things and make my dreams come true. My dreams have changed a little in the last couple of years, but still, you have to have something to aim for, don't you?

For me, New Year's Day is about making resolutions. I am a big fan of making lists because they remind you of what you can do to get closer to your goals. The trick is to stay calm if you happen to mess up; one broken resolution is not the end of the world. If you panic and make a big deal out of it, you are more likely to spin off course. Instead, accept that everyone has blips from time to time and cut yourself some slack. Keep on going! This year, I am making a mood board to help me stay focused; it's an easy, inspiring way to remind myself what I want from the year ahead.

And the final thing I'll be doing on January 1st? I'll be forgiving myself for all the mistakes I made last year; letting them go, and moving on. A new year, a new start. Anything — and everything — is possible!

Summer's Resolutions

1. Eat healthily
2. Keep working hard at ballet
3. Apply to the summer school at Rochelle Academy
4. Check out yoga classes
5. Check out uni courses in creative dance

Mood board

YOU WILL NEED:

- a cork pinboard, or a rectangle of thick card to use as a base
- scissors
- a glue stick
- a stack of magazines, images and photographs

TO MAKE:

1 Flick through your fave magazines to find images you love, then cut them out and collage them on to your pinboard.

2 Add inspirational quotes, pics and photos of friends (I'm putting a pic of Alfie on because he always makes me smile).

3 Pin on small objects that are special to you (my flower hairclip will be on there when I'm not actually wearing it!).

4 Lastly, add your resolution list.

Breakfast Fruit Sundae

You will need:

- 1 handful raspberries
- 1 handful chopped strawberries
- 1 handful blackberries or blueberries
- Greek yoghurt
- clear honey
- chopped nuts, oats or a handful of muesli

To make:

1. Mix all the berries together.
2. In a vintage glass, layer Greek yoghurt, oats, nuts, muesli, mixed berries and honey. Repeat until the glass is full.

A recipe to help with my 'eat healthily' resolution!

147

Your space . . .

MY RESOLUTIONS, HOPES AND
DREAMS FOR THE YEAR AHEAD

Make a Cool Diary or Journal

Cherry says...

I always keep a diary - well, it's more of a journal than a diary because it's not always a record of what has happened each day. Sometimes I just write down my feelings or ideas for stories, or even just special, secret, personal things I don't want to forget.

I am not an artist like my stepsister Honey, but I love doing little manga cartoons in my journal and I add photos and tickets from parties and gigs, anything that means something to me, really. Sometimes I stick things down on the pages of my journal. Other times, I keep them in a special envelope in the back, and at the end of the year I have a whole bunch of happy memories to look back on. I plan to keep the journals to look back on when I'm older. My life has changed so much these last few years - for the better! I want to remember that.

I like to make my own journals, mainly because I don't like the pressure of feeling I have to write something every day and also because some days I want to write loads and loads! It's really easy to turn a notebook into a diary - and personalize it, too! I'll show you how.

YOU WILL NEED:

- scissors
- a piece of thin ribbon
- a plain notebook (I use a
  paperback sketchbook because
  I don't like lined pages)
- sticky tape
- white PVA glue and a glue
  spreader
- a rectangle of wadding a little
  smaller than the cover of your
  notebook
- a fabric offcut a little bigger than
  your opened notebook (iron for a
  neater look)
- coloured paper
- pinking shears (optional)
- a coloured envelope
- sequins, buttons, ricrac or braid
  to decorate

TO MAKE:

1 Snip one end of the ribbon
into a neat point. Lay the
ribbon down the centrefold of the
notebook and fold the other end
over so that it rests against the
spine of the book.

2 Secure the ribbon end there with
a few strips of sticky tape, and
keep the ribbon tucked out of the way
between the pages of the notebook so it
doesn't get caught up in the cover fabric.
This is going to be your page marker.

3 Spread a layer of glue over the front cover of the notebook and press the rectangle of wadding down on this; it will give the front of your new journal a cool padded effect.

4 Lay the fabric right side down on a clean surface. Spread a not-too-thick layer of PVA glue around all four edges of the notebook's front, back and also along the spine. Open the notebook out and carefully lower it on to the fabric, lining up the book and the fabric. Press down firmly, then pick up the fabric covered book and close it gently, to make sure the fabric is a good fit when folded. Smooth down the fabric carefully so there are no bubbles, wrinkles or creases.

5 Now finish off the cover. Use sharp scissors to snip a triangle from each corner of the fabric sticking out beyond the edges of the book cover. Make two more cuts down to the spine of the book. Spread an even layer of glue over the fabric borders and fold them in neatly, one by one. Again, fold and unfold the notebook to make sure everything stays neat whether the notebook is open or closed.

152

6 Cut two rectangles of coloured paper to cover the inside of the front and back covers. I used pinking shears to cut the paper to size because they make a cool serrated edge. Spread an even layer of glue over the paper and stick it down firmly.

7 Spread another layer of glue over the front of the envelope and stick it down firmly inside the back cover to make a pocket to store keepsakes in.

8 You could stitch or appliqué your name on to the fabric at the front, or stitch on sequins, buttons, ricrac or braid.

What to Write About:

✳ Your feelings
✳ Story ideas
✳ What happened at school
✳ Hopes, dreams, fears, crushes
✳ Book reviews, poems, song lyrics
✳ Secrets!

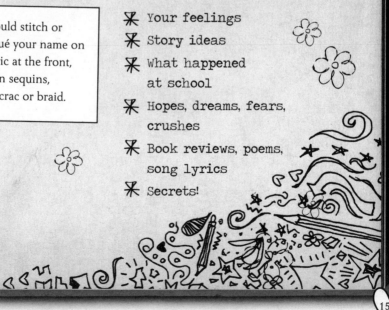

YOUR SPACE . . . .

MY SECRETS

NO-BAKE BIRD CAKE

COCO SAYS...

January is often the coldest month of the year, and that makes it very hard for wildlife — garden birds especially. Feeding the birds in winter is one of the most awesome things you can do, and if you make this special no-bake bird cake it can be fun too. The fat in the cake is really good for the birds in winter and is essential to bind all the dry foodstuffs together. I am willing to make an exception to my usually strict veggie rules and use lard, which is an animal fat, because it's better for the birds and I won't actually be eating any of it myself, obviously. The good thing about bird cake is that, if you don't have all the dry ingredients, it doesn't matter; just use what you can get hold of. The birds won't complain!

YOU WILL NEED:

- string for hanging
- containers: paper cake cases, coconut shells, scooped out orange halves, pine cones (dip them in the mixture)
- breadcrumbs
- lard or suet
- a bowl for mixing
- wild birdseed
- raisins, cranberries or finely chopped apple
- porridge oats
- chopped bacon rind or grated cheese
- peanuts (leave these out if you have a nut allergy)

156

METHOD:

1. Run a length of string through your containers so you can hang up your bird cake when it's ready – leave plenty of string spare!

2. Put all the ingredients except for the lard or suet in a mixing bowl and stir them together.

3. Warm the lard or suet until soft but not totally melted. If you're a beginner in the kitchen, ask an adult to help – hot fat can be dangerous if you get things wrong.

4. Add the warm fat to the dry ingredients and mix thoroughly.

5. You may need to use your fingertips to mix everything in; be brave and think of the birds! Squidge it all together and press the mixture into the containers, or, in the case of the pine cones, roll them in the warm mixture.

6. Place the pine cones or containers on a tray and leave them in the fridge overnight so the fat can set firm.

7. Hang your filled paper cake cases, orange halves, coconut shells and dipped pine cones from high branches or place them on a bird table – out of reach of any cats.

8. Put out fresh water for the birds too, and remember to break the ice on it on freezing days.

COCO'S WINTER WILDLIFE TIPS

♥ If you have a pond, melt a hole in the ice in sub-zero temperatures so that wildlife can still enter the water. Breaking the ice will cause shock waves that can harm smaller creatures, so sit a hot-water bottle on the ice until it melts a hole.

♥ If it snows, look out for wild animal prints. I've spotted fox, badger, squirrel and stoat tracks in the woods beside Tanglewood.

♥ Don't be too tidy in the garden - unpruned plants may look dead in winter, but provide a winter home for insects. Leave compost heaps undisturbed too; frogs, toads and other creatures often shelter there.

157

My 'Happy Things' Jar

Honey says...

In the last couple of years I've had more than my fair share of trouble to contend with, so I plan to start the new year with a clean slate and a positive attitude! This is something I saw online; you get a jam jar and decorate it, and every time something cool happens you write it down on a scrap of paper, fold it up and put it in the jar. The idea is to look out for all those little positive things that we usually take for granted and find tiny bits of happiness in each day. Then, this time next year, you open up the jar and read everything through and, instead of remembering the difficult bits, you remember all the good stuff. How cool is that?

You can use any clean, empty jam jar - pick a nicely shaped one if you can. Soak the labels off in hot soapy water and decorate the jar. Try using a glass-paint outliner to draw some cool shapes; let it dry and fill in the shapes with jewel-bright glass paints! Or try acrylic paints; they work well on glass as long as you don't water them down too much. A simple pattern of spots, flowers or stars would look great. You could tie a ribbon round the neck of the jar or paste on some découpage images - or even just go crazy and collage the whole thing with scraps of bright, torn tissue paper pasted on with thinned-down PVA glue.

See? I am full of good ideas - I really should be an art teacher! (Not!) As for filling it, I've started already!

2015

happy
thoughts
jar

happy

A new year letter from Ash, the coolest boy I have ever known.

Sipping perfect home-made hot chocolate on the window seat in my turret bedroom.

Snow!

The Perfect Hot Chocolate

YOU WILL NEED:

- 1 mug of whole milk (skimmed and soya work fine, but whole milk is my fave)
- a small, non-stick saucepan
- ½ medium-sized, good-quality chocolate bar, roughly grated (I used leftover chocolate from Paddy's workshop)
- a wooden spoon
- squirty cream
- cocoa powder
- a candy cane left over from Christmas, to stir (optional!)

TO MAKE:

1 Pour the milk into the saucepan and place it on a low heat.

2 Add the grated chocolate and stir patiently until the milk heats and the chocolate begins to melt. This is the only difficult bit (patient? me?) but you have to watch milk because it heats very quickly and can boil over or even burn. Get an adult to supervise if you're a kitchen klutz!

3 Once small bubbles begin to form on the surface, take the pan off the heat and pour the milk into your mug.

4 Top with a squirt of cream and a sprinkle of cocoa powder, plus a little grated chocolate and a candy cane to finish.

Serve with a long spoon and a big smile!

WRITE YOUR OWN
HAPPY THOUGHTS

Cool Vintage Collar

Skye says...

Vintage style is a way of life for me, but it's not always easy to dress vintage in winter - at least not when you live in a draughty old Victorian house like Tanglewood, where the heating is always on the blink! Brrrrr!

When the temperature drops, all we want to do is hide away in cosy jumpers and thick woolly tights - it's either that or frostbite. That means my fave vintage treasures often get left in the wardrobe till spring, which is bad news! Luckily I have a solution for adding some quirky vintage styling to those plain old sweaters without actually wrecking them; plus, I get to upcycle old school uniforms at the same time. Perfect, huh?

YOU WILL NEED:

- an old shirt
- fabric scissors
- a needle and thread
- ribbons
- vintage lace
- buttons, sequins, beads and braid

TO MAKE:

1 Carefully cut the collar from the shirt using a pair of sharp fabric scissors and making sure you include the button fastening.

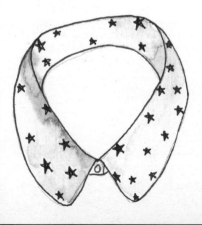

2 Measure a length of ribbon or braid along the bottom of the collar and stitch it on carefully, folding it over to hide the raw edge of the collar and neaten it up.

3 Stitch a length of vintage lace along the collar's edge, or add a layer of thin lace over the top of the collar itself for a pretty vintage look.

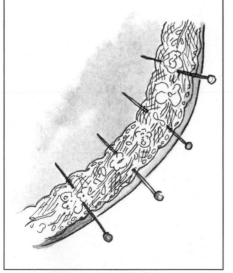

4 Add some quirky style by stitching on a few mismatched buttons near the points of the collar, or stitch on a few sequins or beads for a more understated look.

5 Cut two lengths of ribbon and stitch them neatly to the front edges of the collar; you can tie this in a bow while wearing the collar for an extra-cute look.

163

Your space . . .

DRAW YOUR DREAM OUTFIT

MAKE IT

Valentine's Mobile

Summer says...

With a birthday on February 14th, there's no way Skye and I can ignore Valentine's Day! Forget all the commercial stuff about buying cards and worrying about who might or might not send you one — just see it as a day to help spread love and happy stuff. Last year, the two of us made some cool heart-themed mobiles to hang in our bedroom and share with our friends. They're easy — I'll show you how.

YOU WILL NEED:

- paper and a pencil
- scissors
- paper or card for hearts (I used patterned wrapping paper — small patterns work best. Skye chose photocopies of old sheet music and pages from vintage fashion mags. You could also use coloured card and stick on découpage images of butterflies, flowers, etc.)
- 1–2 metres narrow ribbon or cord
- a stapler or a needle and thread
- a small silver bell (from a craft shop or the haberdashery section of a department store)

TO MAKE:

1 Draw a heart shape (or trace round the template on page 110) to make your template. If you're drawing from scratch, fold your paper in half to make sure your heart is symmetrical! The size is up to you, but a good size is around 12–15 centimetres tall. Cut it out.

2 Spread out the paper or card you want to use, and draw round your template. You will need twelve or more heart shapes. Cut them out carefully.

3 Place the hearts in sets of two, one on top of the other and right side up (if your paper is only patterned on one side). Fold the double hearts neatly down the middle.

6 Staple each double heart to the ribbon using two staples per heart, or use a needle and thread and sew small, neat stitches to secure them. Don't be scared to stitch through the paper; if you're careful and your needle is slim and sharp, all will be fine.

4 Make a small hanging loop at the top of your ribbon or cord; folding and knotting it neatly to secure is the easiest way.

5 Lay your ribbon out on the floor or on a large tabletop, and space your double hearts along it. Take the time to get the spacing right.

7 Thread the tail end of your ribbon through the silver bell and secure it with another neat knot. Your heart mobile is ready to hang.

Ta-dah!

My Secret Valentine

Cherry says...

Don't panic - Shay is my Valentine, and always will be, but on Valentine's Day I like to spread the love a little bit. I am not looking for other boys to flirt with - that's not it at all - but I like the idea of doing nice things for others on February 14th. Think Secret Santa with a February twist - like a kind of Random Acts of Kindness Day crossed with a giant, free-for-all lucky dip!

When I first came to Tanglewood, I was pretty much a loner. I didn't have many friends - OK, I didn't have any. I'd been bullied at my old school and I needed a fresh start, and my new school in Somerset gave me exactly that. People didn't judge me; they gave me a chance, and now, a couple of years on, I have some great friends. So the secret valentine idea is my way of saying thank you to everyone who has helped to turn my life round! Maybe you'd like to try it too?

YOU WILL NEED:

- a list of deserving people
- small gifts to make people smile: tubes or packets of sweets, mini chocolate bars, wrapped toffees, tangerines, badges, hot chocolate sachets, little notebooks, etc. They should all be low-cost, and I collect them throughout the year (except the tangerines)
- gift wrap and labels

WHAT TO DO:

1 Write your secret list of friends, classmates, teachers, family and acquaintances — anyone you'd like to see smile. Wrap your stash of gifts.

LET'S FACE IT: FEBRUARY IS A GREY, COLD MONTH FOR MOST OF US. WE NEED ALL THE HAPPY STUFF WE CAN GET. SECRET VALENTINES ARE MY FAVOURITE THING OF THE WHOLE YEAR.

2 If you have specific gifts for specific people, add a name label.

3 Leave some gifts unlabelled for random or last-minute gifts.

4 Fill a bag with your goodies and start delivering. The trick is to deliver your gifts secretly, without being seen. Try popping a parcel into a pocket or bag, on a school desk or in a locker, leaving it on a doorstep or posting it through a letterbox.

5 That's it! You get to smile to yourself as you see the gifts being opened, and watch the expressions on people's faces — and the confusion as they try to work out who has given them something!

6 Save a few bits 'n' bobs for random gifting — that Year Two kid at the bus stop who's crying because he's cut his knee, the grumpy old lady who lives next door but one — it's up to you. Don't approach strangers, obviously; focus on people you know.

FRIENDSHIP BRACELETS

COCO SAYS...

I am not a fan of Valentine's Day. All that slush and lovey-dovey pink fluffy nonsense; it kind of brings me out in a rash. Well, not literally, but you know what I mean. No, for me, Valentine's Day is just another day of the year. While the rest of the world goes Valentine crazy, I do my own thing and make cool bracelets for my friends!

We've all been through the loom-band craze; here's the vintage version, using embroidery threads. They take a bit longer to make than a loom-band bracelet, but they're super-cool, and eco-friendly too! They also make great prezzies – for Valentine's Day, birthdays or any other day. Here's how to make one pretty simple weave. Once you've mastered this, there are lots of other designs to try – just Google 'friendship bracelets' and see!

YOU WILL NEED:

- **6 strands of embroidery thread in your choice of colours (approx 45cm long)**
- **sticky tape**
- **patience!**

TO MAKE:

1 Knot the ends of the threads together, tape them to a worktop and arrange them in your preferred colour order. Each thread represents a letter in the word friend, so the one on the far left is F, then R, then I, then E, then N, then D.

FRIEND

2 Take the F thread and wrap it over and round the R thread to make a knot. Tighten by holding the R thread and tugging gently on the F thread.

R IEND

Go to www.cathycassidy.com and click the Fun Stuff link to download full friendship bracelet instructions.

3 Make a second knot in the same way; wrap F over and round R to make a knot, and pull on R to tighten.

4 Drop the R thread and pick up the I thread. Make two knots with thread F over and round thread I.

5 Repeat the knots with thread F on threads E, N and D, making two knots on each. Thread F will now be on the right and you will have completed one row.

6 Begin the next row by taking the thread on the left (now thread R) to make two knots over and round each of the other threads – I, E, N, D and F. With each new row, the thread on the left is worked over to the right-hand side.

7 When the bracelet is long enough to go round a wrist, tie a knot at the bottom and snip off any straggly ends. All done!

WHY IS IT CALLED A FRIENDSHIP BRACELET?

Because it's easier to weave if a friend holds the end of the threads for you – though a strip of sticky tape works well too! The idea is to give your finished bracelet to a friend as a symbol of your friendship. You have to tie it on to their wrist, but tie it loosely, as it is bad luck to cut through a friendship bracelet – it's like cutting through the friendship. Instead, tie it so that it can be slipped on and off if need be.

YOUR SPACE . . .

MY BEST FRIENDS AND
WHY THEY'RE COOL

SKYE'S THE LIMIT BIRTHDAY CAKE

Skye says...

This cake has my name on it, but actually it's the invention of my twin, Summer, with a little help from Mum, of course! It's become our traditional birthday cake; it looks sooo beautiful and so impressive with three layers of cakey, creamy, fruity goodness - and it tastes amazing too! I love it because it looks a million miles better than the shop-bought kind of birthday cake. Summer loves it because it's fun to make - and she says that, if you're going to have a blow-out, it may as well be worth it!

YOU WILL NEED:

- 300g caster sugar
- 300g butter
- a large mixing bowl
- 4 medium eggs
- a small bowl
- 300g self-raising flour
- a little milk to loosen mixture if required
- three round, greased baking tins
- a serving plate
- 1 large carton extra-thick fresh cream (or whipping cream beaten until stiff)
- two or three punnets of strawberries, raspberries, blueberries
- a little icing sugar

Add friends and *enjoy!*

METHOD:

1. Preheat the oven to 180°C/350°F/gas mark 4. Mix the sugar and butter in a large mixing bowl until creamy.

2. Beat the eggs in a small bowl and slowly stir them into the butter and sugar mixture.

3. Sift the flour into the wet mixture, stirring thoroughly. If the batter is too thick and solid, add a little milk to loosen; it should be the consistency of thick custard or pancake batter.

4. Divide the mixture between the three greased baking tins.

5. Bake for 20 minutes or until a knife comes out of each cake clean. Remove from the baking tins and leave the cakes to cool on a wire rack.

6. Place one cooled cake layer on to a serving plate and spread it with a thick layer of cream and a layer of fruit.

7. Add the next layer and repeat the cream and fruit layers.

8. Add the third cake to the existing layers and spread with remaining extra-thick cream and fresh fruit. Shake on a little icing sugar if you wish.

175

Your space . . .

PLAN AN IDEAL
BIRTHDAY PARTY

Mocktail Madness

Honey says...

My twin sisters, Skye and Summer, have their birthday this month, and when they were younger I used to invent fun fruit-based punches for their birthday parties. These days they prefer swish mocktails and it just so happens that I am a genius at inventing those too! Perfect for when the adults are celebrating and you want to raise a glass as well - and you want it to contain something a little more interesting than orange squash. They look cool and they taste awesome - what more could you want?

Before you start make sure you have:

• cool glasses – tall, short, stemmed, or an old-fashioned tea set (Skye found one in a junk shop and paid peanuts for it. It's too good to use for tea and makes everything look better)
• cocktail umbrellas (from the supermarket)
• ice (make sure there's a tray or a bag of it in the freezer)
• a blender

Banana Colada

Serves 4

You will need:

• 2 ripe bananas
• 1 cup cubed fresh pineapple
• 1 cup pineapple juice
• ½ cup coconut milk
• 3 cups ice cubes

Method:

Whizz the bananas, pineapple, pineapple juice, coconut milk and ice cubes in a blender. Divide between the glasses and add pineapple wedges to decorate.

Strawberry Dream

Serves 6

You will need:

- 3 cups chopped strawberries
- 1 cup coconut milk
- 1 tablespoon sugar
- 3 cups ice cubes

Method:

Whizz the strawberries, sugar and coconut milk in a blender until smooth. Add ice cubes and blend again, then divide between glasses and serve with a slice of lime to decorate. Tastes like heaven . . .

Fruit Fizz

Serves 6

You will need:

- 2 cups ice cubes
- 2 cups chopped fruit (try apricot, peach, plum and strawberries, in any combination)
- 2 cups peach juice
- 2 cups sparkling drink (lemonade works well)
- 1 cup sparkling water
- a sprig of mint to garnish

Method:

Divide the ice cubes between the glasses. Mix the chopped fruit, juice, sparkling drink and sparkling water and pour over the ice. Garnish with a sprig of mint and a strawberry.

Fruit-tastic!

179

SPR

ING

Who doesn't love spring? Just when you think everything is asleep and the cold, grey, grim days of winter will go on forever, there are new shoots and spring flowers painting colour all around and blossom on the trees. That watery spring sunshine lifts your heart and puts a smile on your face – and suddenly you are full of ideas and enthusiasm again! It's like the world is waking up, and you can't help but wake up alongside it.

Spring is bittersweet for me though, because when the cherry blossom opens I always think of my mum – my real mum, who died when I was little – and I think of what might have been. But mostly it's a glad-to-be-alive time of year, when the months ahead stretch out, full of possibilities and promise.

Cherry♥ xx

Make a Pinboard

Summer says...

OK, I admit it, I like to be organized. I like to know what I'm doing and when, and I like to keep a pinboard with all my important stuff on it. It helps me see at a glance what's happening and what I need to remember; life just runs more smoothly when you don't have to stress about all of that. I suppose that any pinboard would do, really, and you can buy a corkboard cheaply at any discount stationery store, but I like my stuff to look good as well as being organized. It's easy to upgrade a cheap corkboard to a designer pinboard; here's how.

YOU WILL NEED:

- an offcut of wadding
- scissors
- a cheap cork pinboard (from a discount stationery shop)
- white PVA glue
- a fabric offcut (large enough to cover the pinboard and fold neatly behind)
- several metres of ribbon in a contrasting colour
- sticky tape
- drawing pins

TO MAKE:

1 Cut the wadding to fit neatly inside the pinboard frame. Glue it on to the cork surface. This should pad it out so the fabric won't sink below the frame.

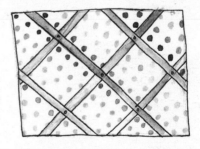

2 Spread a neat layer of white PVA glue on the frame of the pinboard. Spread the fabric smoothly over this.

3 Quickly turn the board over and neatly fold and glue down the raw edges of fabric.

4 On the front of the pinboard, stretch a length of ribbon diagonally from corner to corner, firmly taping and gluing the ribbon ends down on the reverse.

5 Stretch lengths of ribbon on either side of the first one, evenly spaced and attach them to the back in the same way, so that there are three ribbons stretched across the front of the pinboard. Stretch another ribbon from the other two corners, in the opposite direction to the first three ribbons, and attach the ends firmly on the reverse as before.

6 As before, add a ribbon to either side of this central one, evenly spaced and criss-crossing the other ribbons. Attach the ends of the ribbons firmly to the back of the pinboard. Finish the pinboard by pressing a drawing pin into every ribbon cross section.

7 Pin your important stuff or your cool stuff (or both) to the pinboard, or tuck notes, tickets and pictures behind the ribbons.

YOUR SPACE . . .

MAKE A COOL COLLAGE
OF YOUR FAVE IMAGES

Hold a Cake Sale

COCO SAYS...

If there is one thing I care about more than anything else in the world, it has to be animals. Animals are awesome — and we are destroying their habitats and hunting them to extinction. This is just wrong; can you imagine a world without tigers or pandas or elephants, just because people are too greedy and selfish to care that they are being wiped out? Well, I care, and I think you probably do too, and together we actually can make a difference.

Raising money for a charity is fun — and, while you are raising money, you're raising awareness too. I have tried sponsored walks, sponsored car washes, a sponsored swim; I tried a sponsored violin marathon once, but Mum gave me £20 to pack it in so, even though it was sort of a fail, it was a win too! Cake sales are my favourite way to get the cash rolling in, because who doesn't like cake, right? Maybe you and your friends can organize one for a cause you really care about. I'll show you how!

What to do:

Enlist the help of two or three reliable friends, so you can split the work. It's lots more fun if you have help!

DECIDE WHICH CHARITY YOU ARE GOING TO SUPPORT.

Draw up a list of cakes to make, picking recipes that are fairly simple but look and taste good. Try **Cherry Chocolate Fridge Cake** (page 206) and **Flower Surprise Cupcakes** (page 192) from this book — and maybe scones, fairy cakes, flapjacks, chocolate crispie cakes or brownies — whatever you and your friends like and enjoy making, put it on the list. I made panda-face cupcakes when I held my cake sale to raise money for giant pandas; see if you can come up with something creative too.

Prepare:

1. Give everyone one or two batches of cakes to bake the night before.
2. Ask classmates and teachers if they can help too by bringing in a batch of cakes to sell. Lots of people will chip in if they know it will help.
3. Decide whether your cake sale will be just for your class, or open to the whole school — or even hold it at home and get your mum to invite the neighbours.
4. Tell the teachers and your head teacher about the cake sale — if you can have it announced in assembly or morning registration, everyone will know it's happening. Besides, the teachers may buy a whole selection to whisk off to the staffroom.
5. Check with teachers that they are OK with your choices. If they're in the dark about what you're doing, you could end up in trouble.
6. Make posters to advertise the time and place a week beforehand; people need to know where you will be and when. Morning break is a good time; choose a location with room for lots of people to gather and that's not too out of the way.

7. Make a banner to advertise the charity you are raising funds for, and flyers to hand out so people know where their money is going.
8. Price your cakes cheaply: 30p a cake, or two for 50p is a good guideline. People love a bargain!

Make sure you have five or ten minutes to set out your stall before break begins; ask your class teacher (very nicely) to let you out of lessons early.

30p
1 cake
2 for
50p

189

YOUR CAKE SALE POSTER . . .

FLOWER SURPRISE CUPCAKES

Honey says...

At Tanglewood, the cake tin is always full of home-baked sweet treats to lift the spirits after a long day at school, and as we've grown up we've all learned to join in with the baking too. I actually find baking very calming and soothing. Once or twice I have been known to come home from a disastrous party or stomp in after a row with some boyfriend and dig out the mixing bowl, flour, eggs and butter in the middle of the night. Following a recipe is a great way to forget your troubles! Try it and see; it works for me, anyway!

These flower cupcakes are one of my favourite recipes because they look and taste amazing. When I first started making them, I used the cute sugar flowers you can buy at the supermarket or made my own from royal icing mixed with food colouring - and then I discovered that viola flowers are edible. Violas are always in flower in our garden during spring, so I pick a bunch and press the brightly coloured flowers into the buttercream icing - so cute. Perfect for when Coco is having one of her charity cake sales!

YOU WILL NEED:

- 110g butter
- 110g caster sugar
- 110g self-raising flour
- 1 teaspoon baking powder
- 1 teaspoon vanilla extract
- 2 medium eggs, beaten
- strawberry jam
- lemon curd

Try putting viola flowers into ice cube trays and pouring water on top. Then freeze them into extra cool ice cubes for cold drinks. Herbs like thyme and mint work well, too!

Icing

METHOD:

1. Preheat the oven to 180°C/350°F/gas mark 4. Place twelve paper cake cases in a muffin tin.

2. Beat the butter and sugar together in a bowl until the mixture is pale and fluffy.

3. Sift in the flour and baking powder, and add the vanilla extract and beaten eggs. Beat until the mixture is smooth.

4. Spoon into paper cases and bake for 15–20 minutes or until the cakes have risen and look golden brown and firm.

5. Cool for ten minutes, then move on to a wire rack.

6. When completely cool, use a small, sharp knife to cut a small hole in the top of each cake, halfway into the centre.

7. Fill half the holes with strawberry jam and half with lemon curd; the surprise is that you don't know which you are getting!

YOU WILL NEED:

- 110g softened butter
- 220g icing sugar
- ½ teaspoon vanilla extrac
- a little milk to loosen mixture if required

METHOD:

1. Beat the butter until it's fluffy, then beat in the icing sugar a little at a time.

2. Add the vanilla extract to soften the mixture and add a little milk to loosen it if needed.

3. Pipe the icing on to the cupcakes, or spread it on with a knife.

DECORATE:

Add little sugar flowers (from supermarkets) or mould flowers from store-bought royal icing and paint them with food colouring. Or, if you have violas in your garden — and they must be violas, as not all flowers are edible — pick the flowers and pop them on top of the buttercream icing. So cool!

193

Make a Mag!

Cherry says... ♡

When school started a magazine club last year, I knew I wanted to be part of it. I'd love to work in journalism one day; it's my dream job. Since then, we've published four issues of our magazine, and every issue has sold out. It's a brilliant way of getting some writing practice if you're a budding journo like me, but it's also great for artists, photographers, designers and ideas people too. You need a whole team to make a magazine, and the people in that team have become some of my best friends ever. They're so cool and creative - and a lot of fun to work with. Why not start a magazine at your school or youth group? Put some posters up, see who's interested and get started; it's not as tricky as you think, and if it's a school project you have the bonus of a ready-made readership waiting to buy your end product!

YOU WILL NEED:

Creative, arty and organized people – and writers too, of course! These are the jobs you need to fill:

• EDITOR – ideally a teacher, librarian, youth worker or sixth former to keep an eye on the whole project and chase copy when needed.

• ADVERTISING ED – in charge of getting ads for the mag; perhaps £5 for a quarter page, £10 for half and give a discount of £18 for a full page. A few ads will cover the cost of printing the mag on the trusty school photocopier; ask local businesses and the parents of the mag team if they want to take out an ad.

• ART ED – to keep an eye on design, lettering, illustration and that all-important cover.

• FEATURES ED – to stay on top of the feature articles.

• SALES MANAGER – to advertise the mag and organize selling it.

PLUS LOTS OF WRITERS, ARTISTS, PHOTOGRAPHERS AND DESIGNERS.

194

GET THINKING

1 Your mag will need a strong, original and memorable name; get the whole team together and share your ideas until you all agree!

2 Ask everyone to think up feature ideas then pick the best – with a good range of formats and styles. What goes in the mag is up to you.

3 Consider giving your mag a theme, like Christmas, music or back to school, to help give shape to your ideas and features.

4 Plan photo features that include kids from your school or community, such as a school dinner survey with photo interviews, hobbies, fashion spreads with models from school, recipes with pics, makeovers, and so on.

5 Make it interactive: include quizzes, a letters page, even a problem page if you like, and invite readers to submit features, artwork and ideas.

6 GET INSPIRATION FROM YOUR FAVE MAGS; SEE HOW THEY SET THINGS OUT AND WHAT THEY INCLUDE.

7 Find the best talent for your mag – ask art teachers, for example, to suggest people who might be able to design an amazing cover.

PUTTING IT TOGETHER

Your blank dummy will look like this!

1 Meet every week – or a few times a week – at lunchtime or after school. A friendly librarian or teacher may let you use the corner of a classroom and give you access to computers.

2 Don't stress about designing everything on-screen – just print off the words you need and piece everything together in a cut-and-paste way. It looks much artier and cooler, and you can add hand lettering, illustrations, decorative patterns and borders too.

3 Plan the magazine. How many pages will you have? Somewhere between 12–20 pages will work to start with; keep it manageable!

4 Make a list of all the pages and what will be on them. Remember, some ads or features will take up less than a page, and some more. Make a dummy magazine with blank pages that you can use to mock up the features and adjust layouts; it helps you see how everything will look. It takes some skill to put everything in the right place.

5 Your adult editor can handle the printing, or ask whether the school office could do this. Make sure they know which pages need to be printed back-to-back, and let them decide what the print run should be.

6 If you get enough ads, you might even be able to cover the cost of a colour cover – whoop!

7 AS EACH PAGE IS COMPLETED, TICK IT OFF AND STORE IT SAFELY. ONCE EVERYTHING IS READY, IT'S TIME TO PRINT!

8 Once it's all printed, get the team together to collate and staple the mag; then you're ready to sell it.

9 Keep the price low – your ads should cover most of your costs; 50p or £1 seems fair.

10 Sell it at break and lunchtimes and ask teachers and the head teacher to help publicize it; a few posters will help spread the word too.

GO IT ALONE

1. If you'd rather go solo, try a blog. Choose a simple, easy-to-use format (Blogger is user-friendly, but there are lots of options) and post one feature at a time, whenever you can. No worries about printing or selling!

2. If you're confident, try a vlog – film yourself talking about books, hobbies, etc.

For more help, advice and ideas, go to www.cathycassidy.com and click on Fun Stuff to download a fab Make-a-Mag PDF.

197

Hat Tricks

Skye says...

Hats are just awesome. I can't think of many outfits that don't look better with a hat. They're the best ever style statement, and they can be your own personal trademark look as well. Don't panic, I am not suggesting you actually make a hat; I wanted to share my top tips for making vintage-find hats properly fashion friendly.

Obviously, the first step is to get yourself some hats. The good news is that you don't have to scour vintage fairs and retro stores for them, because cool hats are everywhere - in every charity shop, jumble sale and wardrobe. There are great deals online too, if you are an Internet fashionista. Before you buy, go on a hat hunt with some friends and try on lots of different shapes and styles to work out what suits you. Once you've chosen a hat, don't be afraid to customize it to give it a little extra edge.

Beanie Hat

A plain, dark beanie isn't just warm and easy to wear, it can be adapted to suit your mood.

- Add a handful of band badges for emo or indie-band cool.
- Stitch on a fabric patch.
- Add a pom-pom and turn it into a bobble hat.
- Braid some bright chunky yarn to add tassels or plaits.

Chic Beret Hat

Possibly my fave style of hat — seriously, it goes with everything! I am wearing a beret to school at the moment, but I can give it a different look each day.

- ♥ Add a vintage brooch (from a junk shop, or ask your gran) for a boho look.
- ♥ Stitch on a couple of pheasant feathers for a country vibe.
- ♥ Clip on a flower hairslide or corsage.
- ♥ Stitch on some charms or lockets from old or broken jewellery.

Straw Sunhat

I live in straw hats during the summer; a wide-brimmed style suits pretty much everyone.

- ♥ Tie a long silk scarf round the crown of the hat and allow it to hang down behind you.
- ♥ Fit last year's flower crown on a hat for instant festival cool.
- ♥ Stitch a brightly coloured lining to the underside of the brim (do it neatly, folding the raw faric edge under as you go). Then pin back the front of the brim and secure it with a pin to show it off.
- ♥ Thread a metre of rough garden string with pretty seashells and tie it round the hat's crown for a seaside look.

199

Eggstra Cool Easter!

First off, I know that Easter isn't always in April; the date changes each year, but I thought I'd slip this project in here. If you happen to be reading this in a year when Easter falls in March, apologies!

The first thing we do for Easter at Tanglewood is to make an Easter tree; it's usually just branches from the garden, but we decorate it and it sits in the middle of the kitchen table all through Easter. Just go for a walk out in the countryside and cut some spring branches to bring back with you; branches with catkins, buds or blossom are perfect! If you can't get to the countryside, ransack the garden (ask first) or buy some pretty, fake branches from a cheap home store. We have a box of cute Easter decorations we've collected over the years, and you can even cheat and tie on brightly wrapped sweets and chocolate.

My favourite bit of Easter is the eggs, though - and I'm not talking chocolate ones! We hard-boil eggs, paint them and use them for egg rolling; it's an old Easter tradition. We each paint an egg and on Easter Sunday morning we throw them down a slope in the field next to our garden. The one that rolls the furthest without breaking wins, and we usually throw them two or three times until they're all wrecked, then Fred the dog gets to eat them (not the painted shells, though). It's possibly his favourite day of the year!

No good at art? No worries; I have a few techniques that really do work for everybody.

Eggstra Special

YOU WILL NEED:

- a hard-boiled egg
- an egg cup
- acrylic paints
- a small paintbrush
- a jam jar of water

WHAT TO DO:

1 No chicks and bunnies, please — too cheesy! Instead, think stripes, spots, stars and flowers on a plain background. Set the egg in an egg cup and paint the top part of the egg with your chosen base colour.

2 Allow to dry then turn the egg upside down and paint the other half.

4 Once the paint is dry, decorate with horizontal stripes, zigzags, wiggly lines, hearts, criss-cross stars, spots, spirals or flowers. Or you could just write Happy Easter in your best arty handwriting! Acrylic paint doesn't blur or run once dry, so it shouldn't need varnishing. All done!

201

Dye for It

YOU WILL NEED:

- hard-boiled eggs
- a thin wax crayon
- warm water
- white vinegar
- several bottles of food colouring
- 2–3 jam jars
- aluminium foil
- a baking tray
- kitchen paper
- elastic bands of different thicknesses

WHAT TO DO:

1 The eggs must be at room temperature, otherwise the wax won't stick to the shell. With a wax crayon, draw a wandering, swirly line all over your plain, unpainted egg. You can also try criss-cross star shapes, paisley patterns, wiggly stripes or something more complicated.

2 Make a dye-bath: mix ¾ cup of warm water, 2–3 tablespoons of white vinegar and 10–15 drops of food colouring in a jam jar. Place the egg in the jar and leave it for 5–20 minutes.

3 You can double-dip the eggs: make the first dye-bath a paler colour, such as yellow. When you've dyed the egg and let it dry, add more wax patterning on top and dip it in a dye-bath of red or blue.

4 Now remove the wax. Preheat the oven to 130°C/250°F/gas mark 1. Place the eggs on aluminium foil on the baking tray and put it in the oven for ten minutes, until the wax begins to melt. Remove the baking tray, holding it carefully with oven gloves. Pick up an egg in the oven glove and wipe away the melted wax with kitchen paper (take care not to touch it with your fingers – it will be hot). Repeat with the other eggs. Alternatively, you can leave the wax crayon lines on the eggs; they will look just as cool!

5 If you're not feeling arty, tie-dye your egg by wrapping it in criss-crossed elastic bands before dipping it in a dye-bath. When it's dry, remove the bands. No hot wax to wipe away, but a surprisingly cool look!

COOL PATTERN DOODLES

Buttons and Bows

Summer says ...

I am definitely not addicted to vintage like my twin, Skye, but I have to admit that sometimes all that charity shop and jumble sale hunting pays off, and she comes up with some real vintage treasures. Often, Skye's finds might be made from great fabric but have a terrible style or shape; to me, those items are crying out to be recycled into something genuinely cool and pretty.

One really easy way to restyle an offcut of cool fabric is to make a hair bow — a kind of scarf-style hair accessory that looks great with everything.

YOU WILL NEED:

- 85 x 25cm piece cotton fabric (vintage offcut or new)
- fabric scissors
- pins
- a sewing machine or a needle and thread
- 85cm thin craft wire strong enough to hold its shape, but soft enough to cut with scissors (from art or craft shop)
- gaffer tape (from hardware stores)
- old buttons
- a hot-melt glue gun or superglue (get an adult to supervise)
- an old hairslide
- two pieces of thin, gauzy fabric, approximately 10 x 40cm each

Hair Bow

TO MAKE:

1 Fold the fabric in half lengthways, right side in and wrong side out. Use the scissors to taper one end of the rectangle into a point. Fold the fabric over so you can snip the other end into the same shape. You should now have a long, thin rectangle with pointed ends.

2 Pin the edges of the fabric together, checking that the right side of the fabric is on the inside. Using a sewing machine or a needle and thread, stitch neatly along the cut edges of the fabric as shown. Leave a gap of 10cm in the middle of the rectangle.

3 Remove the pins, knot the thread and carefully turn the fabric right side out so that all the seams and raw edges are hidden.

4 Take the wire and fold over one sharp end into a gentle curve, twisting the end neatly to finish. Cover the twist with a patch of gaffer tape. Do the same to the other end so the wire has no sharp ends.

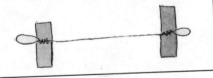

5 Push the wire into the tube of fabric: one end should go up into the point of fabric to the right and the other end to the left. Hand stitch the gap in the fabric closed.

6 Try on your hair bow: it goes underneath your hair at the back, and the pointy ends twist together to make a cool vintage bow to one side of your head – very Minnie Mouse!

Hairslide Bow

1. Cut two lengths of thin, gauzy, chiffon fabric approximately 10 x 40cm. Fray the edges a little by pulling at the lengthwise threads to create a little fringe.
2. Layer the two pieces of fabric one on top of the other; imagine they are one piece, a kind of two-layered gauzy ribbon.
3. Pick up the fabric and tie it in a neat bow. Carefully arrange the loops of the bow, neaten the centre and spread out the tails so all four pieces of fabric trail down.
4. Stitch a couple of old buttons on to the middle of the bow.
5. Glue the bow on to the hairslide.

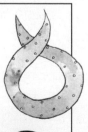

CHERRY CHOCOLATE FRIDGE CAKE

Cherry says... ♥ ♡

We can't all be good at everything. We have our own skills, and mine seem to be daydreaming and writing stories, which is fine with me. It's not easy for me to be part of a big, blended family where everyone else is great at baking, though, because, trust me, I'm not! I am way too easily distracted and more than once I have walked away from the kitchen only to cremate a tray of cupcakes or burn my chocolate brownies to a frazzle. Ouch.

This recipe is my trademark sweet treat; it's a no-bake cake, so even I can't go wrong! Luckily, it's also wickedly chocolatey and everyone loves it. Charlotte showed me how to make it when I first moved to Tanglewood, but the idea of adding cherries was all mine!

YOU WILL NEED:

- 225g digestive biscuits
- a strong plastic food bag
- a rolling pin
- 100g butter
- 200g milk chocolate
- 3 tablespoons golden syrup
- a large heatproof bowl
- a saucepan
- a wooden spoon
- 225g tinned, stoned cherries, drained and chopped
- a baking tray
- baking parchment

METHOD:

1. First put the digestive biscuits in the bag and smash them to small crumbs, using a rolling pin (great way to get over temper tantrums).

2. Place the butter, chocolate and syrup in a large heatproof bowl over a pan of simmering water. Stir with a wooden spoon until just melted.

3. Quickly add the crushed biscuits and the cherries and mix well.

4. Line the baking tray with baking parchment. Pour the mixture into the tray. Put it in the fridge until set. (Overnight is ideal, but it should be ready in a few hours if you are really desperate!)

5. Cut into squares and serve; it tastes far too good to be this easy.

Instead of cherries, use chopped fresh strawberries or raspberries or add mini marshmallows, dried fruit and nuts or Maltesers. Instead of milk chocolate, try dark or white.

Make a Panda Badge

COCO SAYS...

I am campaigning to save the giant panda again at the moment and I'm not just trying to raise money, I want to raise awareness, too. I love making things, so I thought I'd make myself a panda badge. It was really easy and looks so cute — lots of my friends commented on it, which got everybody talking about pandas and how they need our support. I decided to make my friends some panda badges too; why don't you have a go?

YOU WILL NEED:

- tracing paper and a pencil
- fabric scissors
- pins
- squares of white and black felt
- a needle and white and black thread
- black embroidery thread
- two old white shirt buttons
- a small quantity of wadding, kapok or stuffing (cotton wool will do)
- a medium-sized safety pin

TO MAKE:

1 Trace the pattern pieces on page 210 on to tracing paper, and cut them out carefully.

2 Pin the pattern pieces to the felt and cut them out neatly. You should have two white face shapes, two black ear shapes, two black eye patches and one black nose.

3 Pin the eye patches on to one of the white face shapes.

4 Using black thread and small, neat stitches, sew the black eye patches on to the face. Remove the pins. Then stitch the black nose beneath.

5 Using black embroidery thread, sew the white buttons on to the black eye patches, making a cross shape on each button.

6 Pin the two face shapes together, sandwiching the bottom part of the ears between the two top edges of the face shapes.

7 Stitch round the edge with black embroidery thread, using small, neat blanket stitches. Leave a gap on one side of the face.

8 Push a small piece of wadding, kapok or a pinch of cotton wool into the centre of the brooch to give a slight 3D effect, then continue stitching to close the gap.

9 Turn the brooch over and stitch the safety pin firmly to the centre back. Make more stitches than you think you need; this bit needs to be super secure or you could lose your fab brooch.

TEMPLATE
100%

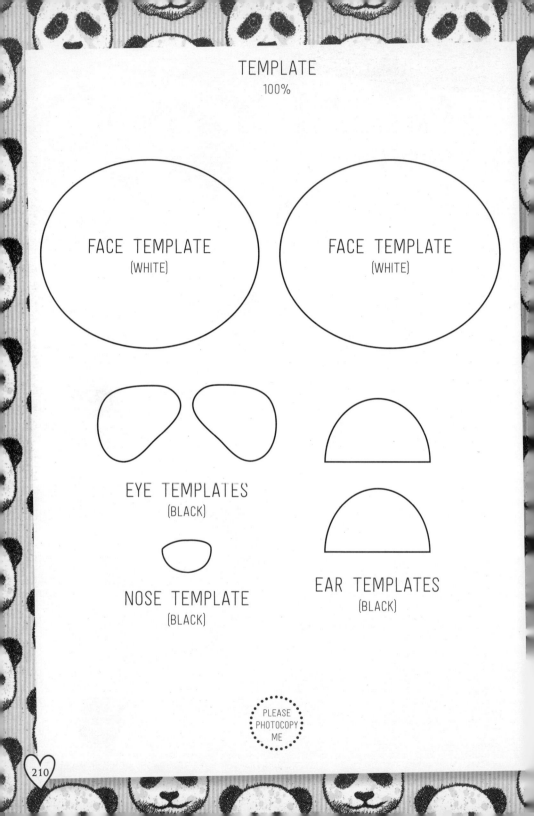

FACE TEMPLATE
(WHITE)

FACE TEMPLATE
(WHITE)

EYE TEMPLATES
(BLACK)

NOSE TEMPLATE
(BLACK)

EAR TEMPLATES
(BLACK)

PLEASE
PHOTOCOPY
ME

DESIGN YOUR
OWN BADGE

Easter Vintage Tea Party

Skye says . . .

This isn't really a Tanglewood tradition, but more a spur-of-the-moment idea. Summer, Cherry and I came up with it this time last year. The three of us had been shopping in Minehead and I had fallen in love with a vintage tea set in a charity shop. We were supposed to be looking for school stuff, but I splashed some of my birthday cash on the tea set.

Some friends from the village were coming over the next day and we decided to throw an Easter tea party, using the tea set and a few mismatched bits and pieces from the kitchen cupboards. We asked people to dress up in something vintage too, and everyone really got into it - it was lots of fun to do. Why not give it a go?

YOU WILL NEED:

- cupcakes, traybake, scones
- teapot(s), a tiered cake stand, milk jug, sugar bowl
- selection of sandwiches with the crusts cut off
- an old embroidered tablecloth and napkins (ours was a charity-shop find)
- vintage teacups, saucers and plates

Prepare:

1 Make invitations in advance and ask everyone to dress up.

2 You can make the cakes yourself the day before, or buy them. You could try making the easy **Cherry Chocolate Fridge Cake** (page 206) or **Flower Surprise Cupcakes** (page 192).

3 On the day, prepare the tea. As well as ordinary tea, try unusual varieties such as Earl Grey and lapsang souchong (it tastes like a bonfire). Put a sugar bowl on the table, fill a milk jug and have everything ready to serve your brew.

4 Make the sandwiches: try egg and mayo, cream cheese and cucumber or tomato and lettuce. Arrange them on plates.

5 Arrange the cakes on plates and cake stands. Lay the table with a pretty tablecloth, napkins or serviettes, knives for butter, teaspoons for sugar and forks for cake, as well as side plates, cups and saucers. It doesn't matter if things don't match; it'll still look amazing.

6 As it was Easter when we held our tea party, we put a tiny foil-wrapped chocolate egg in every empty teacup.

7 MAKE A VINTAGE PLAYLIST WITH LOTS OF 40S SWING, 50S ROCK AND ROLL AND 60S POP!

213

Dress to impress:

I wore one of my fab vintage 1920s dresses and did my hair in a fishtail plait (see page 71). Cherry wore her Japanese kimono and put her hair up with chopsticks. Summer wore a pink chiffony dress that had a vintage feel with a flower clip in her hair. It's up to you how vintage you go!

Time for tea:

When your guests arrive, switch on the retro music, make the tea and get the party started. Take lots of selfies and pics of yourselves in your vintage finery. Imagine you're on the Orient Express or dining out at the Ritz, and have fun! Last year, we ended up inventing mad dances to cheesy 50s and 60s songs, then chilled out afterwards watching the musical *Grease*. This year I think we'll watch *Pretty in Pink*!

Your space . . .

PLAN YOUR OWN TEA PARTY

✳ What will you wear?

✳ Which sandwiches will you serve?

✳ Which cakes will you have?

✳ What songs will go on your playlist?

✳ Which films will you watch afterwards?

Shorts Story

Honey says... I just about lived in shorts when I was in Australia, and they're probably my fave item of clothing even now I'm back in the UK. I have even been known to wear them in deepest winter with thick tights underneath. Shorts go with everything: jumpers, Doc Marten boots, flip-flops, crop tops and T-shirts. You can **never** have enough shorts, but if money is short (isn't it always?) you can make a seriously cool pair of denim shorts from old jeans. What style will they be? That's up to you, but here are some ideas to get you started.

YOU WILL NEED:

- fabric offcuts, red spotted pattern or similar
- fabric scissors
- a needle and thread
- an old pair of jeans
- lace trim
- a bottle of household bleach
- an old washing-up bowl
- an old washing-up bowl
- a thick apron
- 1 cup vinegar
- 1 rubber gloves

Brighten Up Your Shorts

Cover the back pockets with fabric offcuts to give your shorts a new lease of life! Cut two patches of fabric a little bigger than the pockets and hand stitch them on, carefully folding the raw edges under to hide them as you go. Finish the look with a bright scarf threaded through the belt loops. This look works well with turned-up hems; you can line the bottom part of the shorts with offcut fabric so the turn-ups are bright and contrasting.

Simple Frayed Shorts

TO MAKE:

1 Chop the legs off an old pair of jeans; make sure both legs are the same length and cut them longer to start with. You can always make them a bit shorter, but it doesn't work the other way round!

2 Try the shorts on for length; super-short is not a look that suits many, so aim for something in-between.

3 Begin to fray the hems by pulling the threads to create a fringed effect. This can take a while; be patient. Nail scissors can help to loosen the threads. Keep working until the frayed hems are all a similar length – 1cm or more looks good.

In the Trim

Easy-peasy – instead of fraying the ends, neatly hem the shorts and stitch a length of lace trim round the inside of the hem. Simple but cute!

Dip-dye Shorts

TO MAKE:

1 Pour 1/5 bottle of bleach into the bottom of a clean washing-up bowl and top up with water to half fill the bowl. Wearing rubber gloves, lower the shorts into the water so the hem and bottom section of the shorts are underwater and the waistband is out of the water, resting over the side of the bowl.

2 Leave the shorts for 30–45 minutes — longer than this and the fabric may weaken and rip. The bleach will creep up the fabric and lighten even some parts that are not underwater. Put on the rubber gloves again and remove the shorts. Carefully discard the bleach and rinse the bowl (it will be sparkling!), then squeeze out any excess bleach before soaking the jeans in a solution of two cups water and one cup vinegar. This stops the bleaching process.

3 Wash the shorts on their own to get rid of the smell of bleach and allow them to dry, preferably outdoors.

Always wear rubber gloves when working with bleach, and put on an apron to protect your clothing; even a small splash can take the colour out of your clothes.

Your Space . . .

DESIGN A PAIR OF SHORTS

Mystery Book Messages

Cherry says...

I am a bit of a book addict. I love reading and I have a bookshelf of brilliant novels, but I also use the libraries in Kitnor and Minehead as well as the one at school, because libraries are a great way to try a new book or new author totally risk-free. I have discovered lots of awesome new books this way, or by browsing the shelves of 10p books at the local charity shop. Tanglewood is quite shabby chic and also a bit untidy, but in a very arty, creative sort of way. I like my room to be neat and tidy, though, so I often go through my books and set some aside to give away. Giving stuff to a charity shop is cool, but I had the idea of rehoming books I've enjoyed but don't want to keep in a very different way ...

YOU WILL NEED:

- tie-on parcel labels (or make some from string and bright card!)
- a couple of books you've outgrown or want to give away
- curling ribbon or coloured raffia
- clear cellophane party bags
- star sprinkles

WHAT TO DO:

1 Write a nice message on a parcel label to the new would-be owner of each book (I try to make mine funny or cute — see some ideas on the next page).

2 Wrap your book up as if it is a gift, with curling ribbon or coloured raffia tied in a bow (don't wrap it in paper, though; the cover and blurb need to be visible).

3 Tie the label on to the ribbon or raffia so the message is visible.

4 Place the book inside a clear cellophane party bag and add a pinch of star sprinkles (don't worry about the cellophane bag and star sprinkles if you plan to leave your books indoors).

5 Tie the bag closed with ribbon or raffia. Put the books in a bag or rucksack.

6 Take your books to places where the target readership for them are likely to go: school canteen, classroom, youth club, cafe, playground, skate park, train, bus, waiting room, park, etc.

7 Sneak a book out of your bag and put it secretly in a place where someone is likely to find it.

8 Walk away — or, if you prefer, stick around to see if anyone finds the book, but keep it top secret; it's more fun that way!

BOOK SWAP

You can also make a book-swap box at school — a kind of mini-library, where you get to keep what you pick. Ask your English teacher if you can put your swap box in a corner of the English classroom — perfect! Just cover a box with wrapping paper and get friends to contribute a few books to start it off; the idea is that people can pick a book out if they put a book in.

IDEAS FOR

MESSAGE LABELS

- ♥ Take me away from this place
- ♥ Curl up with me!
- ♥ You were made for me
- ♥ I only want to be with you!
- ♥ Free to good home

YOUR SPACE . . . .

DESIGN A NEW COVER FOR
YOUR FAVOURITE BOOK

Use this
space for your
cover ideas
and doodles

Fresh as a Daisy!

Summer says... ♡ ♡ ♡

Right now there are daisies all over the grass at Tanglewood, and that means spring has well and truly sprung!

Daisies are my favourite flower, and I have a cute daisy-patterned skirt and a daisy necklace. I'd have daisy everything if I could! I want to show you my favourite hairstyle, because that involves daisies too – and it means I can pass on my top tips for creating a ballerina bun. It's easier than you think! I also made myself a pretty daisy bracelet not long ago, and that has a ballerina twist too.

Daisy Hairgrips

YOU WILL NEED:

- fabric scissors
- white and yellow felt
- a hot-glue gun or strong glue
- hairgrips

TO MAKE:

1 Cut large circle shapes from white felt, and small yellow circles to make daisy centres.

2 Take the white circles and snip in towards the centre with sharp scissors to create a frilled or petal effect. Add a blob of glue in the centre and dot on the yellow circles.

224

3 Add a second blob of glue on the back of each daisy and press the curved middle of the hairgrip into the glue; allow the glue to harden.

4 *Ta-dah*: daisy hairclips to make spring last all year round! They're quite fragile, like real daisies, so handle them with care.

Daisy Bracelet

YOU WILL NEED:
- white and yellow felt
- fabric scissors
- a hot-glue gun or strong glue, or a needle and thread
- ½ metre narrow green ribbon

TO MAKE:
1 Make a felt daisy as for the hairgrips, but larger.

2 Alternatively, stitch individual white felt petals to a yellow felt centre.

3 Stitch or glue your felt daisy neatly to the centre point of the green ribbon.

4 To wear, place the daisy motif on your wrist and tie the ribbon round your lower arm, criss-crossing it like the ribbons of a ballet shoe; tie in a bow or loose knot and allow the ribbon ends to dangle.

Daisy Braid

YOU WILL NEED:

- a brush and comb
- snag-proof elastic bands
- hairspray
- hairgrips
- daisies

WHAT TO DO:

1 Part your hair in the centre and use snagproof elastic bands to make bunches just behind either ear.

2 Plait each bunch tightly and secure it with more snagproof elastics.

3 Arrange the braids over the front part of your hair, so they cross over each other. Tuck the ends out of sight.

4 Secure with hairgrips. Spray with hairspray.

5 Push daisies into the plaits at regular intervals.

Ballerina Bun with Daisies

YOU WILL NEED:

- a brush and comb
- a snag-proof elastic band
- hairgrips (the long type if you have lots of hair)
- hairspray
- daisies (or buy or make daisy hairgrips for a more lasting look)

WHAT TO DO

1 Brush your hair back from your face until it's completely smooth and then tie it firmly into a high ponytail.

2 Grip the ponytail and twist the hair in your hands from top to bottom; then twist the whole ponytail round in a spiral, securing it with hairgrips as you go.

3 Tuck the end of the ponytail under the bun and add more hairgrips to make sure the bun is secure.

4 Spritz the bun with hairspray to control flyaway strands.

5 If you're not a dancer or prefer a softer look, loosen some tendrils of hair just in front of either ear.

6 Take some daisies (with stalks attached), and push them into the bun at random intervals; a perfect nature-girl spring look!

Jam-Jar Lanterns

Skye says . . .

Spring is definitely on the way, and that means spending more time outside. At Tanglewood we have fairy lights threaded through the trees for most of the year, which I love, but we also have candle lanterns, and they're just magical. They look great when they're plain, but they're also really easy to decorate - and everything looks better by candlelight, doesn't it?

YOU WILL NEED:

- white PVA glue
- a clean, empty plastic yoghurt pot
- tissue paper in different colours
- old glass jam jars, any size and shape, scrubbed clean and labels removed
- an old, cheap paintbrush
- glitter and sequins
- silver or gold embroidery thread
- a coil of thin craft wire (strong enough to hold its shape but soft enough to cut with scissors)
- tealights

TO MAKE:

1 Pour a little white PVA glue into the yoghurt pot. Add an equal amount of water and mix it to a runny consistency.

2 Tear two or three different-coloured sheets of tissue paper into 5–8cm square pieces.

3 Brush the PVA glue on to a jam jar and stick tissue paper pieces on in a patchwork fashion, overlapping them so that all the glass is hidden. Continue the collage, pasting pieces over the neck of the jar and folding them down neatly inside.

4 Brush some glue solution over the tissue paper to make sure that everything is smoothed down. Put one hand into the neck of the jar and, with the other, sprinkle glitter and dot sequins or stars on the outside. You can also wrap a wiggly line of silver or gold embroidery thread round the jar, or curl the thread into spirals. Brush glue over the thread to help it to stick.

5 Allow the jars to dry thoroughly, then take 80cm lengths of wire and place the centre of the wire against the neck of the jar, wrapping it round and twisting it to secure. Curve the loose ends up and over the jar neck to make a hanging wire, twisting the ends tightly round the wire on the other side to secure.

Variation
Handwrite some inspirational words on plain jars, using a permanent marker.

Dreams

Hopes Love

Shine

Shine

Freedom

229

Garden Camp-out

COCO SAYS...

My sisters love sleeping out in the gypsy caravan once the weather warms up. I do too, but camping out under canvas is better still. My favourite way to celebrate the arrival of spring is to hold a camp-out sleepover. My friends love it, even though they're not exactly tomboy types.

Prepare:

1. Pitch your tent in advance. I choose a bit of the garden behind the fruit trees because it's quite private, but any bit of flat ground will do. We have a dome tent, and there's plenty of space for two or three friends as well as me.

2. Make the inside of the tent look good. I usually spread a stripy cotton rug over the groundsheet and scatter some bright, fluffy cushions around.

3. No tent? No worries. Drape or peg blankets or sheets over a washing line or from a whirly clothes dryer to make a grown-up version of the dens you used to make when you were little.

4. For extra magic, we run a long electric cable through the garden and peg some fairy lights up inside the tent, so it's never really dark (note: never have a candle lantern inside a tent – it's way too dangerous).

5. I spread an old futon mattress and duvets in the bedroom area to sleep on; its comfier than the hard ground. Airbeds are another option – see what you can rustle up!

6. Ask your friends to bring musical instruments for a campsite jam – or just plug an MP3 with your fave playlist to the extension lead.

On the night:

The best thing about a garden camp-out is that you have to make your own entertainment; no TV, no laptop. This may sound scary at first, but once you get used to the idea it's fine — promise! Usually, my friends and I eat up at the house, watch a movie then change into onesies and head down to the tent with a packet of chocolate chip cookies and a mug of hot chocolate (see page 160) each. We never run out of things to do and say, but just in case you're stuck I've scribbled you a list.

- Play truth or dare
- Make friendship bracelets (see page 170)
- Do hair wraps (see page 58)
- Paint your toenails
- Tell ghost stories
- Play cards, charades or board games (see page 81)
- Plan a party, picnic or festival
- Sing, play music or do karaoke
- Invent your own fan club for a fave band, book, animal or film
- Write a script and act out scenes from your fave book and film it on a smartphone
- Write a script and act out your own ghost story or horror film
- Invent a spell or ceremony
- Have a midnight feast

Doodle, doodle, doodle . . .

233

Index

Are you a superfan?

Can't wait to discover all the news about Cathy and her amazing books?

Then the brand new

is for you!

Tune in and you can:

▶ Watch video blogs from CHERRY, SKYE, SUMMER, COCO, HONEY and SHAY

▶ See a **NEW** video every time you visit

▶ Enter fun surveys to win **FAB** prizes

▶ See Cathy Cassidy read from her books and answer **YOUR** questions

▶ Watch book trailers, music videos and much, much more!

Visit **www.youtube.com/CathyCassidyTV** today!

Create & Make

BOOK REVIEWS

Dilemmas

Competitions

YOUR VIEWS

Dare to Dream

Be inspired by

Dreamcatcher

Short Stories

The fab **NEW BLOG** from

Recipes

Cathy Cassidy

Creative Writing

DREAMS

BEST FRIENDS

Find BLOG links at *cathycassidy.com*
Or visit cathycassidydreamcatcher.blogspot.co.uk

Catch all the latest
news and gossip from

Cathy Cassidy

at

www.cathycassidy.com

* Sneaky peeks at new titles
* Details of signings and events near you
* Audio extracts and interviews with Cathy
* Post your messages and pictures

Don't Miss a Word!

Sign up to receive a **FREE** email newsletter
from Cathy in your inbox every month!
Go to *www.cathycassidy.com*